BACK ON HER FEET

A LESBIAN ROMANCE NOVEL

NICOLETTE DANE

BACK ON HER FEET

Lucy Burgess has lost it all. At least, that's how it feels. After losing her job in New York City, she's forced to move back to her hometown in Michigan. Living with her mother in her mid-thirties isn't how Lucy imagined her life playing out, and the change is difficult and demoralizing. To Lucy, it feels like a huge step in the wrong direction. And she's finding it hard to get herself back on track.

But there is a glimmer of hope when she meets Aria Caspar, the pretty local barista, a friendly and positive woman in her late twenties, and Lucy's first friend after so many years away from home. While Lucy yearns to put the pieces of her life back together and return to the big city, Aria shows her all the things she has given up to chase her cosmopolitan dreams.

As the two grow closer, amid their blooming romance, Lucy discovers that Aria has her own challenges to contend with. Can Lucy and Aria push through all the loss and heartache together and get back on their feet, or will life's hard knocks prove to be too much for this encumbered pair?

CONTENTS

ABOUT THE AUTHOR

Nicolette Dane landed in Chicago after studying writing in New York City. Flitting in and out of various jobs without finding her place, Nico decided to choose herself and commit to writing full-time. Her stories are contemporary scenarios of blossoming lesbian romance and voyeuristic tales meant to give you a peep show into the lives of sensual and complicated women. If you're a fan of uplifting and steamy lesbian passion, you've found your new favorite author.

www.nicolettedane.com

SIGN UP FOR NICO'S MAILING LIST!

If you'd like to be notified of all new releases from Nicolette Dane and receive FREE books, head over to Nico's website and sign up for her mailing list right now!

www.nicolettedane.com

CHAPTER 1

"**W**ell, here it is," said Jean, pushing open a door. She was in her sixties, with long gray hair back in a single thick braid, a diminutive stature, and a kind face.

"It's so familiar but so different," Lucy remarked. With a duffel bag slung over her shoulder, Lucy stepped into the room and looked around. There was an overstuffed bookshelf on one wall, a wooden desk and an office chair pushed up against another. And in the opposing corner there was a twin bed.

"It's not like you haven't seen it before like this," Jean replied.

"No," agreed Lucy. "You're right. But I guess I'm just looking at it from a different angle now. I'm not just here for the weekend."

"I used it for a home office a bit before I retired," Jean

went on. "But gosh, I don't remember the last time I was even in this room. Well, that's not true... I dusted and vacuumed before you arrived." She smiled.

Lucy moved further into the room, her eyes scanning the surroundings, trying to take it all in. She let her bag fall to the carpet below. This felt like resignation. This felt like failure. This did not feel like home.

"I know it's hard, dear," said Jean. "But please don't feel bad about having to move back home. It's tough out there. There's no shame in needing help. That's what family is for." Jean smiled once again, a kind and understanding smile. After a moment of reflection, Lucy smiled too.

"Thanks, Mom," said Lucy. "I do appreciate you letting me move back. It's been such a hard couple of months. But never at the start of this would I think I'd be coming back to Madeira. It still feels like some crazy dream."

"I think it'll be nice to have you around, Lucy," Jean continued with a longing gaze in her eyes and an absent curl of her lip. "Ever since your Dad died, things have been a bit lonely around here."

"I'm sorry," said Lucy, suddenly feeling saddened and guilty. "I should have been around more. I should have come home more."

"Nonsense," Jean said quickly, snapping out of her reverie. "You were in New York. You had your career and your life. I understood. I'm not upset with you. Now, I'm just glad you're back, if only for a little while as you get back on your feet."

"Thank you," Lucy replied. She smiled softly and let her eyes wander back to the room. This was her childhood bedroom, then it was an office, and now, at thirty-five years old, it would be Lucy's room once again.

"I'll go back to the living room and grab a few more of your bags," said Jean. "The closet is empty and there are a bunch of hangers in there for you. Let's start getting your room organized."

"Okay," Lucy acquiesced with a simple nod. Jean smiled at her, and then she exited, leaving Lucy all alone. As soon as her mother had left, the smile on Lucy's face faded. The reality was starting to sink in. She couldn't believe this was happening to her.

Lucy Burgess looked a lot like her Mom. She was small, with dark brown hair. There were already a few gray hairs punctuating her tresses, hinting at what was to come. Jean had gone fully gray in her mid-forties and Lucy was most certainly headed in the same direction. While Jean was always a gentle and kind woman, Lucy was often described as a firecracker. Lucy was confident and self-assured, she was outgoing and active. But since her life in New York City fell apart, Lucy felt knocked down a peg. Or, more accurately, she felt like she hardly had a peg to stand on.

Moving back to her hometown of Madeira, Michigan was hardly in Lucy's purview. She had never even considered it. After leaving for college at eighteen, she never thought she'd return to Madeira apart from holiday visits. It wasn't that it was a bad place. It was nice enough. It was just a small Midwestern town in Metro Detroit. It never felt big enough for Lucy. It never felt like she belonged.

Madeira had been a stifling place for her when she was growing up. Lucy was just one of two lesbians who had come out in high school. Although she had suspected a few other girls she knew, it was hard being so isolated and that's what Madeira represented to her. It had certainly changed in the ensuing decades, though. Now the town even had a Gay Pride Parade, albeit small. "Madeira's changed a lot," her Mom would often tell her.

But old feelings can sometimes be hard to shake.

Going from New York City to Madeira was a pretty intense culture shock. Sure, Lucy had been back to visit once a year, but now that she was actually living in Madeira, the feeling was wholly different.

Just stepping out of her Mom's ranch home on Elm, a few blocks from Main Street, it was like looking on a view she knew well but with brand new eyes. It was much different than walking out of her building on President in Carroll Gardens, ambling along all those Brooklyn brownstones on her way to Court Street to get a coffee. It was quieter. It was calmer. In New York, Lucy felt like anything could happen. In Madeira, it felt like nothing could happen.

But despite her feelings of inadequacy and disillusionment, Lucy knew she had to make something happen. That something was that she needed to find a job. Being only forty-five minutes outside of Detroit, she focused her search on companies closer to the city. There were, of course, the auto companies and there were a ton of marketing and advertising firms that served them. But in the down economy, the jobs were few and far between. Lucy had been an account manager in advertising for so long, but she had started to realize that part of her career could be coming to an end. She might have to try something else.

On Main Street there was a coffee shop called Fair Grounds and Lucy decided this was where she would go every morning, armed with her laptop, to search job listings and send out her resume. It was a cute cafe, with wood floors, ship-lap on the walls, exposed beams in the ceiling. There had certainly not been anything like Fair Grounds when she grew up in Madeira. In those passing decades that Lucy had been away, Madeira had grown slightly bougie. It was a bit strange, but Lucy was grateful that such a cafe existed so close to her new old home.

As the customer in front of her moved away from the register, Lucy was met by the smiling face of the barista behind the counter. This was a face she recognized, as Lucy had been spending a lot of time at Fair Grounds over the past week. The barista was a pretty young woman, blonde hair back in a ponytail, thick black glasses over her blue eyes, a small hoop pierced in her nose. And although Lucy was undeniably attracted to this chick, she also felt the barista could be a little young for her.

"Double dirty chai latte!" exclaimed the barista, maintaining her smile. Lucy let out a little chuckle and nodded happily in kind.

"You got it," replied Lucy. "I'm surprised you remembered."

"We've been seeing a lot of you," the cute barista said, punching Lucy's order into the small tablet screen in front of her.

"I guess that's true," admitted Lucy, now fumbling a bit with her wallet, fishing around for cash.

"Sometimes it's nice to get out and do a little work at the cafe," the barista went on.

"Hmm?" Lucy intoned, looking up again and handing her payment over.

"Oh, I just mean... you're always here with your laptop," said the barista, feeding the cash into the till. "You seem pretty focused."

"Yeah," Lucy replied carefully. "Pretty focused."

The barista's expression shifted slightly, as though she knew she might have touched a nerve. With a new resolve and replenished smile, she pressed on.

"I'm Aria," said the barista.

"Nice to meet you, Aria," said Lucy, stuffing a few dollars into the tip jar. "I'm Lucy."

"It's nice to meet you, too," Aria said with her bright smile, a beautiful smile that revealed her perfectly straight white teeth. She had the subtlest bit of lipstick on, some shade of nude. Lucy felt her heart race for just a second, and she quickly put a stop to the feelings that were welling up inside of her.

"Thanks," Lucy said shortly, offering a somewhat forced smile. "I'll go..." she continued, thumbing in the direction of the pickup side of the counter. "You know, get my drink."

"Sure," agreed Aria. "Thank you!"

Sitting at her round table in the window of the cafe, Lucy found it impossible to concentrate on her job search. All she could do was look up to the counter at Aria, watch her smile and interact with customers, making small talk and pleasantly accepting money. The infatuation Lucy knew she was feeling made her feel stupid. A lot of her life made her feel stupid lately.

———————

AUTUMN HAD ARRIVED a bit early and Lucy helped her mother rake the leaves that were falling in the yard. She tried to keep busy and active, for in all the downtime she had, Lucy would find herself dwelling on her predicament. It was difficult not to blame herself. But the reality was that there was an economic crisis afoot, and she was just a casualty of that. Her life had been good in New York, and she had felt successful for a long time. It was hard to understand how it had all come down so suddenly.

In a flannel shirt and jeans, Lucy bent down and scooped up as many leaves as she could from the pile. Standing up again, she turned at her waist and dropped them into a tall brown paper bag. Jean, meanwhile, leaned on her own rake and watched her daughter.

"Do you want my gloves?" Jean asked.

"I'm fine."

"Anything on your mind?" pressed Jean.

"A lot," admitted Lucy. "There's a lot on my mind."

"Okay, well..." said Jean. "I'm your Mom. I'm here for you. Here to listen. If you want to tell me, that is."

"There are no fucking jobs," huffed Lucy, rubbing her palms together to clean off any dirt from the leaves. "I look and I apply to what I can, but nobody's hiring right now. Nothing for my experience or skill set. It's infuriating."

"I know, dear," consoled Jean. "I'm sorry. It's not just you, it's everyone. It's a hard time right now. It's been a hard few months. Or, year, really."

"I know that logically," said Lucy. "But it just feels like I'm floundering. I lost everything I thought was my life. I lost my job, my apartment, my life in New York City. It's gone. And now I'm back here in Madeira and it's just..."

Lucy stopped herself, as she could feel the anger rising. She took a deep breath, and then bent down to lift up another pile of leaves.

"Give yourself a break," Jean offered after giving her daughter a few moments to collect herself. "You're okay. You're healthy. You have some money in the bank. And you're back home with me. I'm not charging you any rent. You can use my car whenever you need to. There's food on the table and everything is okay. Just say that to yourself, dear. Everything is okay."

Lucy stood in silence and she let her Mom's words sink in.

"Everything is okay," she said reluctantly.

"There are people out there right now who are not okay," Jean continued. "And we should help them however we can. But you and me, we're okay. You're going to get through this. This is all temporary. It may be painful, it may be long, but it's temporary."

"Thank you," Lucy said quietly. "Mom."

"You're welcome," Jean said and smiled.

The two women continued their yard work, raking and bagging leaves, existing in the somewhat uncomfortable silence. Well, it was uncomfortable for Lucy, as she was living in almost total discomfort for the time being. For Jean, it was fine. She was focused on her task and happy to be spending time with her daughter.

Lucy thought about her Mom's speech. It was true that there was nothing truly wrong. There was a roof over their heads, clothes on their backs, they weren't starving. They weren't really even worried about money. But the assault that Lucy felt was that it was her independence that was under attack. Being back at home, reliant on her Mom, it just made her feel like a child again. And that's what was so difficult about the situation. She was mourning the death of the adulthood she had spent so much time building.

Sitting on her bed, alone in her room, Lucy tried to make sense of what her life had become. Without work to think about, without clients to serve, the hours could only slog by. She had gone from fifty and sixty hour workweeks, dressed in her fancy business attire, feeling important and confident, to feeling like an absolute nobody. It was depressing. Lucy felt worthless. She felt abandoned.

She scanned through her phone for a few minutes, looking at the names of her friends and her colleagues from work, trying to imagine all their lives and where they were ending up. The economic crisis had hit a lot of them, too. Lucy considered calling someone—maybe she could call her friend Heather and see how she and her family were doing —but she just didn't feel up to the task. It was hard to feel excited about sharing her misery.

It felt like there was nothing for her to do. Going from a life wholly dedicated to work to this new life of having nothing to do, it screwed with Lucy's mind. It was making her feel like she was going crazy.

Lucy knew she needed to do something about it. She needed to get out of the house, get out of this mindset, and find some solace somewhere. This room she was in wasn't even hers any longer. All she had was a few bags worth of clothes. The rest of her stuff was back in Brooklyn in storage. Sitting on this twin bed, all alone, Lucy just felt like she needed to get up and run.

And so she did.

ROUNDING THE BLOCK, her house now in sight, Lucy was huffing and puffing as she struggled to make it to the driveway without stopping. She hadn't run since college, and she could definitely feel that lapse in athleticism as she neared the end of her workout. Her body felt soft and squishy. Although she was a woman smaller in stature, years of post-work cocktails and late night hot dogs after the bar had put some additional pounds on her slight frame. When she finally reached her driveway, Lucy came to a stop, she bent over at the waist, and she coughed a few times.

Then, in a very out of character moment, Lucy gathered the phlegm in her mouth in a loud horking sound and spit out a loogie onto the grass.

"Yuck," she vocalized to herself, seeing what she had done. Lucy wiped at her mouth and tried to regain her composure.

Mostly her fancy yoga pants were used for lounging. This run was the first time they had ever been used for their intended sporty purpose. Lucy wiped at her brow and looked around Elm Street to see if anyone had caught her spitting. It was desolate, but for two cars driving by, crossing paths right in front of Lucy's house.

"How do you feel?" asked Jean with a smile when Lucy eventually came inside.

"Like I might die," Lucy replied, ambling to the sink where she filled a glass with water and took a long drink. Jean chuckled.

"Well, you didn't die," said Jean. "So that's good. Maybe this is the start of a new hobby."

"Maybe," offered Lucy with ambivalence, taking yet another drink.

"I didn't tell you," Jean pivoted, looking a bit sheepish in her delivery. "I'm going out with a friend tonight."

"With Georgina?" asked Lucy, referring to one of her Mom's closest friends.

"No, not with Georgina," Jean said. "With another friend. Paul is his name."

"Paul?"

"Yes," Jean confirmed. "Yes, my friend Paul Vonn."

"Is this a... boyfriend?" Lucy queried, lifting an eyebrow.

"Just a friend," Jean quickly clarified. "He's just a friend."

"Huh," said Lucy. She kept her eyes on her Mom as she refilled her glass at the sink.

"I just thought you should know," said Jean. "Because I won't be here for dinner."

"Okay," Lucy said. "That's fine. I hope you two kids have fun."

"Paul is a very nice man," Jean offered. "He's an executive at one of the Big Three. He lost his wife some years ago."

"I'm sorry to hear that," Lucy replied. "About his wife, I mean. It's cool that he's an auto executive. You'd think he'd live in a nicer town, like West Bloomfield or Rochester or something."

"Madeira has gotten really nice," Jean protested. "Haven't you noticed? A lot of people are moving out here. Houses have really gone up in value."

"Okay, I didn't mean to start a thing about Madeira," sighed Lucy. "I hope you have a great time with your pal Paul."

"No need to be snotty," Jean poked with a roll of her eyes.

"You should have seen me outside," Lucy retorted, offering a wry smile.

Jean returned a quizzical look but Lucy just shrugged, took another drink from her water, and exited the kitchen without another word.

CHAPTER 2

*L*ucy sat back in her chair and crossed her arms. She had spent the morning tailoring her resume for a specific job listing and had just hit submit on the web form. However, she didn't get any feeling of satisfaction or completion from this action. It just felt like another resume tossed off into the abyss.

Fair Grounds always seemed busy, even after the early morning rush. The first round of customers were the people stopping in for a coffee on their way to work. Mid-morning was dominated by mothers with strollers, pretty much exclusively in yoga lounge wear, who would hang out for an hour or so with one another. The middle of the day was more of a lunch crowd vibe, people just stopping in for a quick bite and an afternoon pick-me-up. And through the later part of the day, it seemed to be younger people, teenagers after school or twenty-somethings with laptops.

Seeing this predictable transition of customer types made

something begin to click in Lucy's mind. Her Mom was right. Madeira was changing. It certainly wasn't as cosmopolitan as New York—how could anything be?—but it wasn't the same place Lucy had come of age. It had grown from its small town roots and had experienced a new influx of obvious wealth.

With an empty mug, Lucy approached the counter during a lull in customers and was met by that cute barista Aria. Aria smiled pleasantly at Lucy and Lucy smiled back. She placed her mug on the counter.

"Another of the usual?" Aria asked knowingly.

"I don't know," Lucy replied, looking up at the menu. "I was thinking of trying something else."

"Ah," intoned Aria with a raised eyebrow. "Just let me delete my assumption off the screen here." Lucy chuckled softly.

"What's your drink?" Lucy asked. "Do you have a favorite?"

"I love the green tea latte," said Aria. "It has an amazing creaminess to it."

"I'll take that," Lucy quickly decided. "A large."

"You got it," Aria replied, making a few quick taps on the screen.

"This place is always so busy," pivoted Lucy, trying to satisfy her intrigue. "I mean, even during this economic downturn, people are still coming in here and buying five dollar coffees."

"Economic issues like we're seeing affect people in different ways," Aria opined. "There are a lot of people with money in Madeira. It's sort of become a rich suburb, you know?"

"Yeah, I suppose it has," said Lucy with a distant look in her eyes. "Have you lived here all your life?"

"No, I grew up in Southfield," Aria said. "When I was in college, my parents moved to Madeira. After college, I moved back in with them and here I still am." She laughed and shook her head.

"So you still live with your parents," mused Lucy. "That's all right. Post-college can be a weird time of trying to find your place."

"I've been out of college for eight years," Aria said and laughed again. "I'm twenty-nine." Lucy's eyes widened.

"You're kidding?" Lucy blurted, immediately feeling embarrassed by her candor. "I mean, I'm sorry... you just do not look twenty-nine to me. I thought you were a lot younger."

"That's okay," Aria said with a smile. "I'll take that as a compliment."

"Well, look," Lucy continued. "Don't feel bad or anything. I'm thirty-five and I'm living with my Mom again. My whole life has come crashing down on me. It's a mess." Lucy leaned against the counter and pondered her existence. Her quick little daydream ended with a sigh.

"I'm sorry to hear that, Lucy," said Aria. "Still no luck in finding a job?"

"No," Lucy replied softly, feeling increasingly bad about herself. "Nobody seems to be hiring."

"We are," Aria said matter-of-factly. "Fair Grounds needs another barista."

"What?" said Lucy, with a quick chortle. "I appreciate that, but I'm a... you know, a professional. I just don't think it's a good idea to take a step back like that... no offense."

Aria made a suspicious face, and Lucy tried to interpret it.

"You can make some pretty decent money here," Aria offered. "We split tips, but it can add up over a shift. And that cash in the tip jar is tax free. It's not bad for a part-time job and maybe it could get you through your current predicament."

Now Lucy looked at Aria suspiciously, attempting to figure out why she might want to convince Lucy to work there. It felt as though there was a battle of wits going on. But that could have just been Lucy's corporate competitiveness peppering her experience. Maybe Aria was trying to make her own escape. Or maybe she was just trying to help.

"I'll think about it, okay?" Lucy said after a moment.

"Oh yeah, no problem," replied Aria. "You do you. I was just offering. Hey, you're here enough!" With this Aria laughed.

"Yeah, I definitely am," agreed Lucy.

"It looks like your green tea latte is ready," Aria said with a smile, pointing down toward the pick-up counter.

"Oh, all right," Lucy said, just now remembering that she had placed an order. "Thanks Aria."

"You got it!"

Lucy looked at Aria for a moment and then she walked down the counter toward where her drink sat. Her latte was in a large squat white mug, still steaming from its preparation. Aria's coworker, a bearded guy that Lucy knew was named Adam, had been the one who made the drink for her. Behind the counter and finishing cleaning the milk steamer, Adam caught eyes with Lucy and saluted her with two fingers at his temple. Lucy smiled weakly at him as she held her drink.

A strange sensation percolated through Lucy, and she couldn't stop herself. Walking back to Aria's side of the counter, drink in hand, Lucy once more approached the barista.

"Hey," Lucy said.

"Hey," replied Aria with some confusion. "Everything okay? Is the drink all right?"

"Yeah," affirmed Lucy. "Yeah, it's fine. Listen. Do you want to get together and talk sometime? Maybe get a drink?"

"A drink?" said Aria, letting out a small laugh. "Like a coffee?"

"I don't know, sure," said Lucy. "Or a beer or wine or whatever. Just to talk."

"Well, I don't drink alcohol," Aria said. "And I don't know how enthused I'd be coming here to work on a day off..."

Lucy felt supremely embarrassed, as it felt like Aria was turning her down. But just as Lucy was about to speak up and tell her to forget it, Aria pushed on.

"But yeah," Aria agreed, smiling in earnest. "I'd definitely like to get together sometime and just... talk."

"That's great," said Lucy, a smile coming over her face. It was the first time in a while she had felt like she had a win. "That's just... really great."

"Here," said Aria. She pressed a button on the receipt machine on the counter, releasing a strip of paper. Ripping the paper from the machine, Aria scribbled on it with a pen and then handed it over to Lucy. "That's my number. Give me a text sometime."

"Cool," Lucy cooed as she accepted the paper and looked down into it. "I will." The paper had 'Aria Caspar' written on it, along with her phone number.

Lucy smiled once again and pushed the paper into her pocket, after which she resumed holding her mug with both hands. There was now a silence between the two, both standing there with a smile, even though it was a little awkward.

"I'm gonna go to my table," Lucy said finally. Aria let out a laugh.

"Okay," said Aria. "Enjoy the latte."

"Thank you," Lucy said. "Thanks."

ARIA LEANED into her kitchen counter and carefully picked apart a rotisserie chicken into small pieces. Some of the pieces went into a glass storage container, while others went onto a white plate with an ornate floral design pattern around its rim. There was duty written on Aria's face as she accomplished her task, her movements methodical as though she had done this many times before.

After finishing with the chicken, Aria scooped a few spoonfuls of a sweet potato mash from a larger bowl onto the plate. Once she knew she had enough of the mash, she left the spoon on the plate and put a piece of cellophane over the bowl. Now with a composed plate of food in front of her, Aria stepped back from the counter, crossed her arms, and sighed deeply.

In the adjoining living room, an old man sat in a deep, cushy chair with a blanket over his legs. The television was on and the volume was turned up. A game show was on, a large spinning wheel of prizes circled around the screen. The old man's eyes were pointed at the large glowing screen, but it looked almost as though he was looking right through it.

Aria entered the living room with a small smile, carrying a tray with the plate of food on top of it. She approached the man, who was old enough to be her grandfather, and she lowered the tray down onto his lap.

"Here you go, Dad," said Aria. "Dinner's ready."

The old man looked to her for a moment with no change in expression. Then he looked down to the plate of food, and then back to the television.

Aria hung there for a moment in silence, looking between the man and the screen. Her smile remained.

"Okay, then," she said after another few beats of silence. "Enjoy."

Back in the kitchen, Aria began cleaning up. She put the leftovers in the refrigerator and she used a wet rag to wash up the counter. It was a nice kitchen, with modern appliances, white cabinets, and a veined granite counter top. She put the kitchen back together in silence, focused on her work.

But her flow was interrupted by the opening of a door some steps off from the kitchen. Coming in from the garage was a woman of about sixty. She wore a gray pantsuit, black heels, her hair blonde and short. This woman looked very put together and confident. When she entered the kitchen and saw Aria, she smiled.

"Hello, sweetie," said the woman. Her name was Phyllis.

"Hey, Mom," Aria replied.

Phyllis waltzed into the kitchen past Aria and approached the other end of the counter. She took her large bag from her shoulder and dropped it to the counter. Then she removed her phone from inside of it and hooked it into a charger that was already plugged into the wall.

"Did you have a nice day?" Phyllis asked.

"Not bad," said Aria.

"That's good," replied Phyllis. "Did you feed him?"

"He's eating dinner now."

"Thank you," Phyllis conferred. She then fished through her bag once more and removed a leather folder from it. Opening it up on the counter top, Phyllis pulled a few papers out and looked through them.

Aria remained there in silence for a minute or so,

watching her Mom sort through her paperwork. Phyllis looked up at her.

"Sorry," said Phyllis. "I've got to get this offer in for a client. We're hoping someone doesn't swoop in with a cash offer, so I must submit this as soon as possible."

"There are some leftovers in the fridge if you're hungry," intoned Aria.

"Thank you, dear," said Phyllis with a flat smile. "I think I'm just going to retreat to my office to finish things up. I'll see you in a little while."

Phyllis closed her folder of paperwork, gave Aria one last smile, and then scurried off from the kitchen and disappeared down the hall. Then, just as quickly as she had disappeared, Phyllis reappeared and approached the counter where she had just stood.

"I almost forgot my phone," she said. Phyllis yanked the charging cable out of her phone, and then she once more made her escape.

Aria looked around the kitchen again. The sounds of her Dad's game show could be faintly heard from the other room. She felt achingly lonely.

SITTING cross-legged in a large leather chair, Lucy swiftly typed into her laptop while her eyes darted from the small screen to the much larger television screen across the room from her. She was fashioning an email to a friend in New York, an email with the purpose of fishing for a potential job. It was a long shot, this Lucy knew, but she was throwing everything at the wall to see if something would finally stick.

Lucy paused from her work to look up at the television once more. On screen was a fashion runway scene, with a panel of judges talking about the design presented to them. Lucy smiled and watched for a moment, listening to the judges' critiques and how it compared to her own thoughts about the dress the model was wearing. Her thoughts were interrupted by the opening of a door at the front of the house.

After a few moments, Jean entered the living room. She wore a black coat that ended at her knees, and black boots that approached her knees. Her hair was up in a composed bun with two chopsticks. She was a very well put-together older woman, with an obvious artistic side to her. Jean looked to the television and then over to Lucy and she smiled.

"So?" asked Lucy. "How was the date?"

"I had a great time," said Jean. "Paul is a gentleman. And a very nice conversationalist."

"Am I ever going to get to meet him?"

"Maybe," Jean weighed. "I just don't want to jump the gun." Lucy laughed.

"It's not like you'd be bringing him home to meet you teenage daughter," quipped Lucy. "You don't have to emotionally prepare me to meet this guy. I can take it, Mom." Jean gave her a look.

"I did tell him I have a thirty-five year old daughter living with me at home," said Jean.

"Oh? And what does he think about that?"

"He asked if you needed around the clock care," Jean admitted. "I was tempted to say yes."

"Okay, Mom," said Lucy. "That's enough."

"I told him you had lost your job in New York," Jean quickly rerouted. "And that you were just spending some time at home to get back on your feet. He understands. His brother's son is in a similar predicament."

"Well, I'm glad you had fun," said Lucy. "I hope to meet this Paul someday."

"Did you have a good night?" asked Jean as she began removing her earrings.

"Just watched some TV," Lucy replied. "Worked a bit on my computer. Nothing too exciting."

"I've been telling you," started Jean. "Contact some of your old friends from high school. Maybe they're still around Madeira. You never know what kind of friendship you might rekindle."

"I don't think I want to be friends with someone who never left Madeira," Lucy snarked. "Can you even imagine?"

"You are such a snob, Lucy," said Jean. "There's no need to be so catty."

"I am not a snob," countered Lucy. "Just a realist."

Jean shook her head in disapproval. She then began unbuttoning her coat as she turned from the living room and started to walk away.

"I'm telling you," she called from the other room. "You really ought to look for some friends. Maybe even try to go on some dates. It'll help keep your mind off of your job situation."

"I am looking for friends," Lucy called back. "Just not people I went to high school with. In fact, I might have found someone new to hang out with."

"Oh?" Jean said, now popping back in with piqued interest.

"Yeah," Lucy admitted, shrugging it off as though it weren't a big deal. "I've been talking with this barista at the coffee shop. She seems nice. I think we might try to hang out soon."

"Really?" said Jean with a growing smile. "That's very nice, dear. I think you should."

"She even told me that I should consider working at the coffee shop," said Lucy with a scoff. "Can you believe that? But besides that, I think she—"

"You should," Jean interrupted.

"What? Should what?"

"Work at the coffee shop," said Jean. "It'll keep you busy, put a little money in your pocket. Lucy, I think it's a great idea. If they're hiring and have a spot for you, I'm sure you'd get it. You're an outgoing woman. You'd be a shoe-in."

"Yeah, but Mom... that feels like such a huge step back for me," protested Lucy. "Besides, how would my resume look to potential employers with 'barista' on it? Not good."

"So you don't put it on your professional resume, Lucy," said Jean sternly. "This isn't a career. This is a job. With the uncertain economy, it would be very beneficial to have some additional income. You don't want to completely drain your savings."

"Right..." mused Lucy as her Mom's words began to sink in.

"I highly suggest you consider it," Jean confirmed. "Give that barista a call or stop in and see her tomorrow and get an application. Just do it and don't think too hard about it. Even if it's just one or two days a week, it's something. You'll feel a lot better if you're out there working a little bit."

"Hmm."

"Think about it," Jean said with finality, tapping at her head. "I'm turning in for the night. Just sleep on it."

"Okay, I will," agreed Lucy.

"Goodnight, dear," said Jean, offering her signature smile.

"Night, Mom," said Lucy.

She watched as Jean left from the living room, and as soon as she was gone Lucy grabbed for her phone from the side table next to her. She scrolled through her contact list and looked for Aria's number. And then she found it. Aria Caspar. She looked at it for a moment, thinking about what her Mom had said. Lucy also felt an attraction pulling her toward Aria, some kind of romantic feelings welling up within her for this girl. Lucy couldn't deny that there was a mild infatuation going on.

But she stopped herself. Lucy quickly put her phone back from where she had gotten it, and took a deep breath as she closed her laptop. There was no need to be impulsive just because her Mom had suggested it. Instead, Lucy decided to give it a bit of time. Besides, it was probably too late in the evening to text someone she barely knew.

Still, it was something she continued wrestling with later into the night. It would have been nice to have a connection with someone. This unemployment was driving Lucy crazy.

CHAPTER 3

*D*ressed in her running attire—a half-zip long sleeve shirt and leggings—Lucy walked down Main Street with a packet of papers in her hand. She felt nervous, embarrassed, and a little bit sad all at once. There as a chill in the air, though the sun was out. When she approached the door to the coffee shop, Lucy deeply sighed, steadied herself, and entered.

There was no line at the counter, and as Lucy walked up to face Aria, she pushed a smile onto her face. Aria brightened up when she saw Lucy approach.

"Morning, Lucy!" beamed Aria. "Are we making a dirty chai latte today or what?"

"Not today," replied Lucy, her eyes darting away for a second. "I'm actually just dropping this off." She handed her packet of papers over to Aria.

Aria took the papers and looked down into them. She immediately knew what it all was.

"I came in last night and picked that up from Wendy," offered Lucy. "I just decided... you know... maybe you were right." Aria smiled and nodded in approval.

"I'll make sure she gets it," said Aria, holding Lucy's application aloft for a moment before and turning around and sticking it into a cupboard behind the counter.

"Just so you know," continued Lucy. "I put you down as a reference. I hope that's okay." Aria laughed.

"What? Really? You put me down as a reference?" she repeated.

"Yeah, I did," said Lucy. "I know we don't really know each other that well, but I figured... hey, we're friendly enough. I said we were 'budding friends' as our relationship." Aria laughed once again.

"I'll vouch for you," she said, still smiling, and offering Lucy a wink. Now Lucy chuckled.

"Thank you," Lucy replied. "I really appreciate it."

"Wendy likes me a lot," said Aria. "So my word goes a long way. Unless you've got any felonies on your record, I think we can make this happen for you."

"No felonies," Lucy confirmed. "I just hope my work history doesn't look too strange."

"I think it'll be fine," Aria counseled. "So hey, if you're not posting up at your usual table today and tickling your laptop, what are you doing today?"

"Well," Lucy started, motioning down to her attire. "I'm about to go for a run. Then I'll probably shower and then eat a little something. Then I'll spend the rest of the day trying not to dwell too much on my messy life." Aria grinned.

"What do you think you're doing around, say, one-fifteen or so this afternoon?"

"Oddly specific," Lucy retorted. "I have to say that I don't really have plans for one-fifteen as of yet."

"I'm off at one," Aria clarified with a smile. "Why don't you and I meet in Central Park around one-fifteen to just, you know, have a chat? I'll bring a couple of dirty chai lattes for us."

"Central Park?" repeated Lucy, feeling a bit confused and lifting an eyebrow.

"Yeah," said Aria. "The park downtown here. You've been to Central Park before, right?"

"Oh!" Lucy said, suddenly understanding. "Yeah. Right. Central Park. I was totally thinking about New York. That's the Central Park I know best."

"Yes, our Central Park here in Madeira is quite a bit smaller," teased Aria. "But it does share a name with its more famous counterpart."

"I'm sorry," Lucy said, shaking her head and feeling embarrassed. "So... one-fifteen in Central Park?"

"That's right," Aria replied. "What do you think?"

"Yeah," agreed Lucy. "That's great. I'll meet you there."

"Perfect," said Aria with her blue eyes twinkling through her black glasses. "I'll see you then. And... I'll make sure Wendy gets your application. She should be in around noon or so."

"Thanks Aria," Lucy said. "I really appreciate it. And I'll see you later on."

"Awesome," Aria beamed. "Have a good run."

"Thank you," praised Lucy. "Thanks." She gave Aria a small wave and a weak smile, and then she made her way toward the door. Aria watched Lucy's exit, the authentic smile remaining on her face.

THE REST of the morning found Lucy in a state of heightened anxiety. Her run helped a bit, but the thought of meeting with Aria put some stress on her mind. Lucy didn't feel like her best self, and as much as she wanted to sit down and talk with Aria, maybe do a little flirting and see where things went, she just wasn't sure she was up to the task. Having fallen from such a high pedestal, even if only in her own mind, Lucy felt bruised. She felt ugly.

As their presumed meeting time approached, Lucy considered texting Aria to call it all off. But that felt silly. Aria knew Lucy had nothing going on. How childish would she look if she made up some excuse not to attend a simple meeting in the park? Instead, Lucy threw open her closet and searched for the perfect outfit. Her instinct was to yank out something professional-looking, maybe a nice floral blouse and some black slacks. But that felt so out of place. It felt like it belonged to a past life.

Dressing appropriately for the season, Lucy ended up in a chunky knit sweater, a pair of brown herringbone leggings, and some ankle boots. She put her dark hair into two braids, and she went light on the makeup. As she prepared, this whole thing felt like a date. But Lucy couldn't be sure. Her interpretation of reality felt out of whack. Nothing really felt quite right.

Lucy arrived in Central Park early. This Central Park was, of course, nothing close to what she was used to in New York. Here, there was a covered area of picnic tables, a playground, a small basketball court, and a river running off to one side. Trees surrounded the park on two sides, and the final side was the road, a continuation of Main Street. The parking lot was half full. Sitting atop a picnic table out in the open, butt on the table and feet on the bench, Lucy felt strangely like she was in high school again. Nostalgia came washing over her.

She was so deep in remembering her past that she didn't notice her new friend walking up, a paper cup in each hand. Aria wore her usual bright smile as she came upon Lucy and Lucy, feeling startled as Aria suddenly appeared to her, shook her head and woke from her trance.

"Whoa, there you are," mused Lucy. "Sorry, I was totally just spaced out." Aria laughed and handed a drink over to Lucy.

"That's okay," said Aria. She was dressed in sneakers and jeans, and wore an over-sized gray hoodie on top of her work shirt. Her blonde hair was up in a bun, with a few tresses of it falling out haphazardly.

"Mmm," hummed Lucy, enjoying a sip of her drink. "That's good."

"I thought I'd try your drink today," said Aria, holding her own cup up for a moment. "It's not bad!"

"It's been my favorite forever," admitted Lucy. She watched as Aria stepped up onto the bench and sat down next to her on the picnic table. With one hand in her hoodie pocket, Aria tipped her cup back with the other and took a drink.

"I gave your application to Wendy," Aria said. "I think you'll get it. We really need another hand around there to cover some shifts. It's actually been tough finding someone."

"That's so weird to me," said Lucy. "You'd think in such bad economic times, you'd be getting hundreds of applications."

"Yeah, I don't know," replied Aria. "I don't understand it. I think it's been a lot of white collar job loss, you know? And a lot of those people don't often look to service industry jobs."

"It feels like a step back," offered Lucy.

"Hmm," intoned Aria. "Yeah, I can see that."

"You work really hard to get some place in your career," Lucy went on. "And now you're back where you were when you were a teenager."

"It's not all that bad," Aria countered. Lucy immediately noticed her misstep.

"I'm sorry," said Lucy. "I didn't mean anything by that. It's just, I mean—"

"No, I get it," Aria said, slowly nodding and then taking a sip from her cup. "I'm not offended."

"I'm sorry," Lucy said again. She just wanted to crumple

up. Aria noticed Lucy's change in posture, she smiled softly, and she placed her hand on Lucy's back.

"Really, it's okay," cooed Aria, still smiling. "I'm not offended. I like my job at the coffee shop."

"It's been a hard year for me," Lucy admitted. "Really hard."

"Do you want to talk about it?" asked Aria carefully. "You don't have to. But if you want to, I'm happy to listen."

Lucy looked at Aria for a moment in silence, wondering if she should open up to her. They hardly knew each other, but Aria had been pretty nice to her and she seemed like a good person. And it was nice to feel like Lucy was making a friend here in Madeira.

"First," said Aria, holding up a finger. "I'm going to open up to you so that you feel more comfortable with me. How does that sound?"

"Yeah, that's okay," said Lucy, already feeling her comfort level with Aria grow.

"Okay," Aria continued. "Cool. I'll be straight with you. I think you seem like a good person, and when you asked me the other day if I wanted to get a drink sometime, I got really hopeful. Hopeful that maybe we could be friends. I don't have many close friends. My life is kind of complicated and..."

Aria paused as she picked her words, trying to maintain her smile the whole time. Lucy watched her with empathy.

"And... well, I could really use a friend," Aria conferred.

"I don't have any friends here in Madeira," said Lucy. "So yeah, I would love to be your friend. Beyond my Mom, and some other family, I don't really have any friends in Michigan at all."

Aria's smile was authentic. There was real happiness printed on her face.

"I just feel so stupid ever since I lost my job," Lucy went on. "I know it's not my fault, but I feel like such a loser. I lost everything. I don't know how it happened. It was like... everything was okay, everything seemed fine even though I knew the economy was tanking all around me... and then all at once, bam!" As she said this, Lucy smacked her palms together.

"I think that's how it happened for a lot of people," consoled Aria. "My Mom works in real estate and it's been a bumpy ride for her. Weirdly, house sales haven't slowed down as much as you might think during a time like this. People are losing their houses, but there are others who are right there to snatch them up."

"I was just renting in New York," said Lucy. "And thankfully I was near the end of my lease. So I didn't have that kind of headache to deal with."

"What did you do in New York?" asked Aria. "What was your job?"

"I worked in advertising as an account manager," said Lucy. "Basically, I was responsible for facilitating my firm's relationship with clients, bridging the gap between the client and creative, bringing in new clients, all that. It was a sales role, more or less, and I earned commission on top of my salary. It could be high pressure, but it was also high reward."

"Did you enjoy it?"

"Definitely," Lucy said with confidence. "I felt really suited to it. It made me feel important. And the money was really nice."

"The money won't be as good at the coffee shop," replied Aria with a hint of sarcasm in her voice. Lucy let out a small laugh.

"Yeah, I know," said Lucy.

"But it's a fun job," continued Aria. "The people are generally nice. It's a good atmosphere. And hey," she said, holding up her drink. "Free coffee."

"I know it's temporary," said Lucy. "But right here, in the thick of it, it feels like the end."

"So why did you come to Madeira?" asked Aria. "You had your life in New York. Couldn't you have stayed there?"

"My apartment was expensive and I didn't want to blow through my savings," Lucy said. "I didn't have anyone I could move in with. I spent the remainder of my lease, three months, trying to find a job with no luck. It was just an emergency pressure release. I put all my stuff in storage and I headed back here."

"Do you think you'll go back?"

"I want to," said Lucy. "I apply to jobs out in New York, but everything is so messed up right now. Nothing's happening for me. It's so disheartening."

Aria just nodded in understanding. It was a beautiful autumn day and a gust of wind blew some fallen leaves past them. Lucy sat there, cradling her drink, staring down at the space between her feet on the bench. The more she talked about her situation, the worse she felt. It felt good to get it out in the open, but it also made her feel like a fool.

"You'll figure it out," Aria offered. "Don't worry too hard about it. You're not alone in your situation or in how you feel."

"Thanks," said Lucy. She looked at Aria and then she looked down to her coffee. She took a sip. The foolish feeling was still there, but it was nice to have Aria sitting next to her. It felt comforting to have a new friend.

"LEVEL THE GROUNDS and then use this to tamp the espresso down into the portafilter," Aria said with focus on her face, watching as Lucy followed her instruction.

"Like this?" Lucy asked.

"Yep, but give it just a little more pressure," corrected Aria. "Not too much, because you want the water to be able to push through the espresso."

"Okay," said Lucy, taking all of Aria's words into consideration.

"That's good!" Aria offered with a smile. "You want the espresso to be even in the portafilter or else you'll get an uneven extraction. And that can mess with the flavor."

"So I put it on this thing?" asked Lucy, moving the portafilter closer to the espresso machine.

"You got it. Just fit it into the machine, and turn it to lock it in place," Aria taught. "Then we'll place the mug underneath and press this button here."

"All right," Lucy said skeptically. "Here goes nothing."

Lucy pressed the button that Aria had pointed to and the espresso machine came to life. It growled and whirred and soon enough, creamy brown espresso exited from two openings on the portafilter. Lucy watched with a curious smile on her face. It was her first time making espresso for herself.

"That's great," said Aria, giving a little golf clap. "Like a pro. Now unlock the portafilter and knock the puck of grounds out into this bin here. You might need to give it a bit of force."

Lucy nodded and did what she was told, unhooking the portafilter and then knocking it onto the bin. After a couple of hard knocks, the puck of expended coffee dropped out and crumbled among other pucks that had come before it.

"Now clean the portafilter and dry it," Aria conferred. "Give it a quick rinse here in the sink and dry it off with this towel."

"That wasn't as difficult as I expected at all," mused Lucy, once more doing as she had been instructed. Aria laughed.

"No, it's not bad," she said. "You just want to make sure you've got a fine grind on the beans, you level off the grounds, and you give it a nice, firm tamp down. Soon enough, it'll all just be muscle memory. Easy peasy."

"Terrific," said Lucy, her smile growing with her accomplishment. "I made espresso."

"Now let's learn to steam milk properly," said Aria,

placing her hand delicately on Lucy's shoulder in cama-raderie.

AFTER HER FIRST shift at Fair Grounds, Lucy was feeling spent. She wasn't used to being on her feet at work. And even though her shift had only been six hours, her feet and her calves were implying to her that it had been far longer. The work, mixed with her newfound interest in running, combined in the exhaustion she felt.

Lucy sat at a table alone and drank a chai latte, still wearing her black apron with the Fair Grounds logo on it. She was lost in her own ruminations, trying to figure out how she got here. In a strange way, this didn't feel like her life. It felt as though she were now inhabiting the life of someone completely different.

Her daydream was interrupted by the smiling face of Aria, who approached Lucy's table with happiness exuding from her aura. She held her own mug of coffee. Pulling out the chair opposite from where Lucy sat, Aria lowered herself down and placed her mug on the table.

"Great job today," she said. "I really mean that. Especially during that rush we got around eleven. You were picking out pastries like a madwoman." Lucy laughed, feeling a sense of accomplishment.

"Thanks," said Lucy. "When all those people starting to come in, I really felt panicked for a second there. But you were a total boss the way you corralled them and orchestrated it all. I was so relieved when you took charge."

"It's just experience," replied Aria. "I've been here for two years, I know everything about it, I know a lot of the customers. Don't worry. You'll get there."

"Well, I hope I'm not here for two years," said Lucy, immediately feeling embarrassed by her words. "Ugh. Sorry. That came out wrong." Aria laughed.

"Don't worry," she consoled. "I know what you mean. I'm not offended."

"Sorry," Lucy said once more. "It's just... this is temporary for me."

"I know," said Aria. She nodded slowly, smiling, and then took a drink.

"So what now?" asked Lucy.

"We're finished for the day," Aria said. "Free to run around and do what we please."

"I'm not sure what I'm going to do," mused Lucy. "I should probably apply to some jobs. But it would feel kind of weird going home to get my laptop and then coming back here." Aria chuckled and grinned.

"Yeah, I can see that."

"What are you going to do?" Lucy posited.

"Me?" said Aria. "Um. Well, I'm going to head home and make my Dad lunch. Then... I don't know yet. I'm in the middle of this project, organizing my room and getting rid of stuff. You wouldn't believe it, but I still have so much stuff from my childhood. I've decided it's time for it to all go."

"Yeah," Lucy absently agreed. Then she paused. "Make your Dad lunch? Can't he do that himself?"

"No," said Aria simply. "He's older and struggling with dementia. I take care of him."

"Really?" said Lucy. "I didn't know that. Didn't you say you live with both your parents? Doesn't your Mom take care of him? Or is she older and ill, too?"

"Um," intoned Aria, averting her eyes for a moment. "My Mom is a bit younger than he is, and she's fine. But... well, taking care of my Dad really isn't on her to-do list."

"Oh," offered Lucy. "I see."

"It's okay," Aria continued. "I don't mind it. I love my Dad and I just feel it's my duty to take care of him in his old age."

"That's very kind of you, Aria."

"Yeah," said Aria. "Yeah, so I should actually get to that." Taking another deep sip from her mug, Aria stood up once more.

"Do you want to get together again soon?" Lucy asked. "Outside of the coffee shop?"

"Sure," Aria said, brightening up again, if only for the moment. "Just shoot me a text. I'm down."

"Great," Lucy said, smiling. "I will."

"Great," Aria repeated. Then she paused. "Okay, talk to you soon. Awesome job today."

"Thank you," replied Lucy.

Aria offered one more smile and then she turned from Lucy's table and walked away. Lucy watched as Aria carried her mug back up to the counter and handed it off to Wendy, the manager of Fair Grounds. They had a quick exchange before Aria left the conversation and made her way to the door. Before she exited, Aria turned and looked across the cafe to Lucy. She smiled and waved, and Lucy smiled and waved back. And then Aria was gone.

CHAPTER 4

*S*ipping on a glass of wine, her laptop open on the kitchen table where she sat, Lucy was lost in thought. It was another night alone at home. Jean was out with her boyfriend, so Lucy couldn't even commiserate with her mother. The loneliness was really beginning to set in and bring her down. It was getting tiresome.

Lucy picked up her phone and fondled it absentmindedly. Looking through her contact list, there were so many people but somehow very few of them felt like actual friends. Ever since she lost it all and moved back to Madeira, her phone had been silent. Nobody had called to check on her to see if she was doing all right. Lucy justified it by thinking that all her friends had their own problems to worry about. Many of them had lost jobs, too. But it still hurt.

Landing on one of her closest friends back in New York,

Lucy stared into the phone screen for a lingering moment and meditated on whether or not she should reach out. It would be nice to hear Sarah's voice, and maybe Sarah would even have a lead on a potential job. After some internal back and forth, Lucy hit the call button and put the phone to her ear.

It took a handful of rings before Sarah picked up.

"Hey lady!" beamed Sarah from the other end of phone. "It's been so long."

"I know, right?" replied Lucy with forced enthusiasm. "How have you been?"

"Oh, you know," Sarah offered. "Just trying to keep my head above water." Sarah paused, and then her voice changed to hold more empathy. "How's Michigan?"

"It's okay," replied Lucy. "It's weird. But I'm making do."

"Yeah?" said Sarah. "That's good. You're a resilient woman, Lucy. I know you got this. You'll be back in the game before you know it."

"Right," mused Lucy, unable to hide her disappointment. "How's your job?"

"I mean, things are slow," said Sarah. "But I'm thankful I'm still employed. There was another round of cuts but I made it through."

"Well, that's good to hear," Lucy conferred. "Your company isn't doing any hiring, are they?"

"No," Sarah said. "No, I'm sorry. We're on a hiring freeze."

"Yeah, I figured," said Lucy. "I just thought I'd ask. I

haven't had any luck here in Michigan. It's been brutal. I actually took a part-time job at a coffee shop."

"Oh yeah?" replied Sarah. "Hey, at least it's something."

"It's something," repeated Lucy. "It gets me out of the house, at least."

"Are you looking for jobs in New York?" asked Sarah. "I mean, are you trying to get back to the City?"

"I am, and I am," affirmed Lucy. "But everything is such a mess right now. And seeing as I'm not even there any longer, it's a much harder search."

"Oh, I'm confident you'll be back here before you know it," said Sarah. "You got this. Just keep looking and applying and I'm sure something will come your way eventually."

"Thanks," Lucy said.

"But hey," Sarah continued. "I actually can't really talk right now. I'm about to step out. It was nice catching up with you though, and we should have another call soon when we've both got more time."

"Yeah, okay," said Lucy. She couldn't tell if she felt brushed off because Sarah actually was brushing her off, or because she felt under attack most of the time lately. Lucy gave Sarah the benefit of the doubt.

"Keep on it," Sarah offered firmly. "I believe in you."

"Thanks," said Lucy. "I'll talk to you soon, Sarah."

"Most definitely," replied Sarah. "Have a great night, Lucy."

"Thanks," Lucy repeated. "Bye."

"Take care!"

And then Sarah was gone. Lucy felt even more alone

after the call. It was such a short interaction with so little substance. But Lucy knew Sarah had her own life to attend to. She had a husband and a daughter. Friends like Lucy fell to the wayside after a while. Lucy was beginning to realize how little she herself had. When she was younger, she just knew that by the time she hit her mid-thirties, she'd have it all. But now that she had arrived, it didn't even feel like Lucy had a friend she could talk to.

Lucy rolled her phone in her palm a few times as she let these thoughts stew in her head. Her thoughts were self-loathing and toxic and she just felt so damn bad. Why did this all happen to her? How did it happen? Lucy had played by the rules, she had done everything right. Hadn't she? She didn't even know anymore.

Picking up her wine glass, Lucy slammed the rest of it down with a gulp and a wince. Maybe she should just go to bed. At least sleep would be an escape from this spiraling reality.

DRESSED in joggers and chunky fleece sweater, Aria sat upright in her bed, back against the wall, with the television on. She watched a cooking competition reality show with half-interest. It was a long-running show that she had enjoyed, but for some reason her attention span was failing her. Looking out of the window into the dark autumn evening, Aria felt lonely.

Escaping from this life of servitude felt like a far-away

dream, even more so now with the economy as messed up as it was. Aria had put it in her mind that she would stick around Madeira and take care of her Dad until his inevitable departure, after which she'd go somewhere else and do something else. But that somewhere and that something weren't clear. She had no real work experience beyond the service industry. And while she definitely enjoyed what she did, it just didn't feel sustainable.

With the way the world looked, even after her Dad died, Aria would probably still remain living in this house and working at Fair Grounds. It could be worse, but she had always hoped it would be better.

Aria picked up the remote and paused the show. She had missed the last few minutes anyway, lost in thought. After some consideration of rewinding the stream, Aria instead decided to shut it off. She exited the show and she powered off the television, tossing the remote down onto her bed.

To assuage the boredom and distraction, Aria picked up her phone and scrolled through it. She immediately knew staring into that black mirror wasn't the answer. It was never the answer. It just made the time fly. In the past, Aria spent a lot of time on social media, but she had grown tired of it. Especially so during this economic crisis, with political opinions flying. She had unfollowed most people and instead focused her online attentions on cute cat pictures. But even that had run its course. There was very little her phone offered her anymore.

Aria felt obstinate out of nowhere. She felt disappointed

and distressed. Ever since meeting Lucy and helping her get the job at Fair Grounds and being nice to her, Aria felt for sure she had been making a new friend. They had both even talked of hanging out, but beyond a few casual things at the coffee shop, there had been no hang out. Aria wondered if maybe she had come on too strong, or perhaps Lucy was just being nice and didn't really care to be friends outside of work. Aria wished it could be different. She could use a friend.

Resolved to give it one more try, she initiated a text message with Lucy and swiftly typed into her screen with her thumbs. She had a look of concentration on her face, her tongue poking just slightly out of her mouth. Aria didn't even have to think for a moment about her words. It all just came naturally.

"We both have tomorrow off," Aria typed. "Do you want to go to the cider mill for cider & donuts & a pumpkin or 2?"

She read it over once and then hit send. Aria watched her phone for a few beats, waiting to see if Lucy would respond, and when that response didn't come immediately she tossed her phone aside and collapsed down onto her pillow.

It was hard being so positive all the time. Tonight, Aria just felt beaten down and tired.

With her face buried in her pillow, feeling sorry for herself, Aria's enthusiasm quickly re-energized when she heard her phone sound off with a ding. She jolted upright and reached for it, excitedly looking into the screen. Her eyes widened.

"I haven't picked a pumpkin from a pumpkin patch in like two decades," Lucy's text read. "I think that would be fun. Let's do it."

Aria's heart warmed and all the negativity that had been brewing inside of her melted away. That person wasn't her anyway. Down times didn't define Aria. Because it was the up times that made her feel alive.

""Yes!!!" was Aria's text reply. "I'm excited. I'll pick you up around 11, does that work?"

"Sure!"

"We're on! This place has got the best donuts. You'll love them. Hope you're having a great night!"

"Thx! See you tomorrow."

Aria fell back down in her bed and clutched her phone happily. It felt nice to have a friend. It had been a while.

WHEN ARIA PULLED up into Lucy's driveway, Lucy smiled to herself as she assayed Aria's car. It was an older, very utilitarian-looking tan luxury sedan. It was still in nice shape, and it wasn't the kind of car that Lucy imagined that Aria would drive. Opening the passenger door and sliding in, Lucy offered Aria a gentle smirk.

"Nice car," she said. Aria grinned.

"It's my Mom's old car," said Aria. "Like, two cars back.

She's a real estate agent, so you know... she's got to look successful." Lucy laughed.

"It's kind of like an old lady car, isn't it?" teased Lucy. Now Aria laughed and enthusiastically nodded.

"Yeah, it feels like that," she said. "But the leather interior is nice and I love this moon roof." Reaching up, Aria gave the glass of the moon roof and few taps with her nail.

"All joking aside, it is a nice car," offered Lucy with a smile as she fastened her seat belt. "I don't even have my own car. I'm sharing my Mom's with her. I can't believe I'm thirty-five and I'm sharing a car with my mother. My life is circling the bowl."

"It's not that bad," replied Aria, now looking into the rear view mirror as she reversed out of the driveway. "Things are just different these days. Life isn't as straightforward as it used to be."

Lucy looked over at Aria and smiled calmly. She was right.

The drive to the cider mill was relaxed and easy. The two women had no problem getting along. There was something similar about them, despite their differences, and they could both feel it. Everything just felt natural and right.

"I'm not used to this slow lifestyle," admitted Lucy. "Everything in New York is so fast. You're always rushing around. You're rushing to work in the morning, and then you're busy all day, then you're rushing out for a cocktail. You get home around eleven and rush through your evening routine, and then do it all again the next day. Now that I'm back in Madeira, I don't even know what to do with myself."

"Lately I've been watching a lot of TV," Aria said. "It's not the most fun I've ever had, but it takes my mind off of a lot of stuff."

"Yeah, TV doesn't fill the hole I'm talking about," replied Lucy. "There's just something else about the City. Something alive. You feel it every day when you're there. I feel like I'm missing something being so far away from it."

"Hmm," intoned Aria, biting her lip. "Well, southeast Michigan isn't as glamorous as New York City. But it has its beauty. I don't know if I could ever feel comfortable rushing around like you say."

"I don't know if anybody ever feels comfortable doing it," Lucy conferred. "But it just feels like you're a part of something bigger than yourself."

When they drove up to the cider mill, Lucy felt a smile grow over her face. Although she had never been to this particular place before, the whole thing was just as she remembered cider mills to be. There was a big red barn with crates of pumpkins and gourds in front of it. People were wandering about, picking up those wrinkled orange globes, surveying which might make the best jack-o-lantern. The scene flooded Lucy with nostalgia.

The girls decided they were going to walk the fields and find their pumpkins out there. It was a beautiful sunny day, with a nice crisp breeze in the air. At one point in their walk, Aria had gotten ahead of Lucy. And when Lucy looked up to find her, she felt her heart beat resonate throughout her body. Aria was standing there, about twenty feet in front of her. She was dressed in dark blue skinny jeans and black ankle boots, wearing a red and black buffalo plaid wool jacket. Her blonde hair was up in a bun, and her black glasses were stark against her pale face. Aria hoisted a pumpkin up, turned to look at Lucy behind her, and smiled big.

That's when it hit Lucy for real. She was falling for Aria.

"I found mine!" called Aria, now holding her pumpkin up higher. "Look at it. It's perfect!"

Lucy just kept smiling and nodded.

Sitting across from one another at a picnic table, each with their chosen pumpkin on the seat next to them, Lucy and Aria sipped on cider and snacked on warm doughnuts. To Lucy, the experience was one of the most wholesome things she could remember doing in a long time, and now that she felt this burning inside of her for Aria, she couldn't help but give in to it all. The cider mill, the pumpkin patch, Aria, the comforting chill of a pretty autumn day, it filled her with happiness. It was a happiness that Lucy hadn't felt in a while.

"I'm not sure what comes next for me," mused Aria. "I know that working at Fair Grounds isn't forever. But my sociology degree hasn't really lead me anywhere, either. I'm not in any rush. Once something happens to my Dad, though, I know I'm going to have to make some moves."

"You don't think you'll stay in Madeira?" asked Lucy. "You won't stay with your Mom?"

"I really don't know," Aria wavered. "I do like Madeira. But I don't think I could keep living at home. My Mom and

I aren't really on the same page. Things are just weird with her."

"Like how?"

"How?" repeated Aria. She thought about the question and took a sip of cider. "Well, she's just too involved with herself. She's never been a very warm woman. And with my Dad's health issues, she's just retreated even further. It's like she doesn't care about him all that much." When Aria said this, Lucy could feel the sadness.

"I'm sorry to hear that," offered Lucy. "My Dad died of a heart attack. He was only fifty-five. That was just five years ago."

"That's awful, Lucy," Aria replied with empathy in her eyes. "That's really rough."

"I wasn't around as much as I should have been during that time," said Lucy. "Sometimes I feel like I really let my Mom down. I probably should have moved home for a while then and helped her out."

"I'm sure your Mom understands," said Aria. "You had your life in New York, your career. It's hard to drop everything."

"I know," Lucy said. "But still."

Aria offered a soft smile as she reached across the table and took Lucy's hand. Lucy looked to her, and smiled as well as they both squeezed.

"Thanks for bringing me here," Lucy went on. "I really needed this."

"It's great, isn't it?" replied Aria with a revived happiness. "I love coming here in the fall."

"I can't wait to carve our pumpkins," added Lucy.

"Let's do it really soon," Aria proposed. "Like tomorrow night."

"Where should we do it?" asked Lucy. "At your parents' house or mine?" With this, they both laughed.

A real friendship had bloomed.

CHAPTER 5

The next night, the plan was for Lucy and Aria to meet up at Lucy's house to carve their pumpkins. In preparation for the get-together, Lucy spread newspaper out across the dining room table. She also mulled some cider on the stove top, but left the brandy out of it because she knew that Aria wasn't really a drinker. As she prepared for Aria to arrive, Lucy felt a deep desire to impress Aria. She wanted everything to be perfect.

The doorbell rang and jostled Lucy from her hostess focus. She grinned wide and raced to the front door. Upon opening it, she was met with a similarly smiling Aria, wearing the same plaid coat from the day before, with her pumpkin in her hands.

"Come in, come in!" Lucy said, stepping out of Aria's way as she motioned for her to enter. Aria stepped inside and looked around at the house, surveying where Lucy lived for the first time.

"Thanks," offered Aria. Without a word, Lucy reached out and took Aria's pumpkin from her. Aria smiled happily and then begun removing her coat.

"Get settled and I'll take this into the other room," said Lucy. "Just follow me when you're ready."

"Okay," said Aria, now hanging her coat up on a coat rack. She looked around again at the house. It was a nice ranch from the 50s, nothing fancy. It was actually a lot more humble than Aria had expected from the way it looked outside. Her own home, decorated by her mother the realtor, was updated and modern. But Lucy's home probably hadn't changed much in a couple decades.

As Aria crept into the kitchen, following in Lucy's footsteps, she saw Lucy at the stove, using a ladle to fill two mugs with hot cider. Aria approached cautiously as she absorbed this new environment.

"Here," Lucy said through a smile, handing over a stoneware mug to Aria. "It's mulled cider, the cider I picked up at the mill yesterday."

"Mmm," intoned Aria, looking into the steaming cup.

"I left out the brandy," said Lucy. "But I think I may add a little to mine."

"You know, I'll take some," said Aria. "Just not too much."

"Yeah?" replied Lucy. "Okay, cool."

Lucy took the mug back from Aria and placed it on the counter next to hers. Then she picked up the bottle of brandy, unscrewed the top and splashed some in to each mug. Finally, she picked up a small spoon and stirred, mixing Aria's drink first and then her own.

"If I start to make a fool of myself," began Aria. "Please stop me." She laughed, and Lucy smiled.

"I doubt you'll make a fool of yourself," she replied.

"If you say so," Aria teased. She grinned and took a sip, wincing slightly from the alcohol.

"Is there a reason you don't drink?" Lucy asked carefully.

"Yeah," said Aria. "I went a little too wild in college. I stopped completely my senior year and haven't really had a drink since."

"Oh my God," Lucy replied, feeling guilt move through her. "I'm so sorry. I'll get you a new mug. I don't want to push anything on you if it's a... you know... problem, or something."

"No, no, no," Aria said, putting up her palm and smiling. "I'm fine. Really. It's not a problem, I swear."

"Are you sure?"

"Positive," Aria confirmed. She smiled and took another sip.

Not too much later, both Lucy and Aria were elbow-deep in their pumpkins, yanking out the stringy orange guts and white seeds. The light over the table was warm, not too bright, and comforting. There was a small speaker sitting on a hutch against a wall with music coming from it at a low volume. Attached to that speaker was Lucy's phone.

"I want to make my jack-o-lantern look like a powerful witch," Aria conferred, stepping back slightly from her work to look at her pumpkin and determine where the face should go. Lucy laughed at her friend's description.

"A powerful witch," Lucy repeated. "I like that."

Just then, Lucy's phone sounded off with a ding. She stopped what she was doing and wiped her hands off. Then she waltzed over to the hutch and picked up her phone. Aria watched with interest.

Lucy looked into her phone screen for moment, her lips flat as she thought about what she was reading. Nodding to herself slightly, she then quickly typed a message out, hit send, and replaced her phone where it had previously laid.

"Everything okay?" Aria asked cautiously.

"That was a text from my Mom," Lucy replied. "She's out with her boyfriend Paul tonight. She said not to wait up for her." Aria laughed.

"Seriously?" said Aria. A small smile started to grow on Lucy's face.

"Yeah," Lucy confirmed. "This is all so weird. Like, the roles are reversed somehow. But yet I'm the kid living at home. I just don't get it."

Lucy put her hand on her forehead, and when she took it away there was a small bit of pumpkin guts sticking to her. Aria noticed it immediately, she laughed, and she pointed to her own forehead.

"What?" said Lucy, watching Aria mime.

"You got something," Aria clarified, again pointing to her own forehead. "Right here."

"I do?" posited Lucy. She reached to her forehead and touched it, quickly discovering the pumpkin. Picking it off, she brought it forward and looked at it, making a face. "Ew."

Aria laughed once more.

"Well, good for your Mom," Aria offered. "Sounds like she's having a fun night."

"I guess she is," said Lucy, wiping at her forehead once more to make sure it was totally clean.

"I'm pretty sure my Mom goes out with other men," Aria said, reaching once more into her pumpkin to pull out a gooey mess.

"You think she cheats on your Dad?"

"Yep," said Aria matter-of-factly, dropping pumpkin guts down onto the newspaper. "He's out of it. She's still young. I mean... what are you gonna do?"

"Right," mused Lucy absently.

Aria smiled gently and shrugged.

"I think I could use a refill," Aria said after another moment, motioning to her empty mug with her head.

"Coming right up."

IT HAD GROWN LATER into the evening, and after the pumpkins were carved and everything was cleaned up, Lucy and Aria ended up on the couch each with another mug of mulled cider in their hands. They had a large throw blanket shared between them, and the warmth was comforting on a chilly fall night. Lucy could feel a growing closeness with Aria, though she was uncertain that she wasn't just projecting her own feelings onto her. The way Aria looked at her, though, Lucy really felt there was something there.

"Are you getting worried about your Mom, yet?" Aria asked with a hint of teasing in her voice. She the pushed her glasses up her nose slightly and took a drink of cider.

"I don't think she's coming home," offered Lucy. She picked up her phone and looked at it. No new texts.

"Well, so then... are you actually worried?" said Aria, her tone changing slightly. "I didn't mean to make light of it."

"I'm not worried," said Lucy. "She's a grown-ass woman. I know she can take care of herself."

"Have you met her boyfriend yet?" Aria questioned. "Paul?"

"I haven't."

"Has she told you anything about him?"

"Yeah, I mean... he sounds fine," said Lucy. "Like I said, I'm not too worried."

"Good," said Aria with a reassured smile. She paused. "I have to pee."

Lucy laughed and accepted Aria's mug as she handed it to her.

"Go pee," said Lucy, turning slightly and setting Aria's mug down on the end table.

Grinning, Aria began unwrapping herself from the throw and stood up from the couch. But as she stood, one leg was still tangled up in the blanket and without much warning, Aria tripped over herself and stumbled down onto the floor.

"Aria!" called Lucy, tossing the blanket off of herself

and bolting up. But by the time she had dropped down to the floor to check if Aria was okay, Aria was already laughing. Lucy smiled wryly and began laughing herself.

"I'm a klutz," offered Aria with a shrug and a smile. Both girls were on their hands and knees on the carpet, sharing a moment of joy. And in that moment of joy, there was an undeniable happiness surging between them. Their laughter subsided into simple smiles.

And then, with a deep and knowing grin, Aria leaned forward and kissed Lucy on the lips. Surprise overtook Lucy and shock painted her face. But that shock quickly dissipated and very suddenly the girls were delicately and excitedly kissing each other.

It was a tender moment of love and friendship, and it was something Lucy hadn't felt inside of her for a long time. In such a dark time of her life, there was now light. This passion gurgled up within her and she redoubled the passion with which she kissed, releasing her tongue and pressing her mouth firmer to Aria's. Aria pulled back and laughed once again.

"Hold on," said Aria, stifling her own giggly excitement. "I still have to pee." This admission brought Lucy back to Earth and she laughed as well.

"I'm sorry," Lucy offered. "Go pee, go pee."

"But I want to continue this," Aria confirmed, holding a palm out as she picked herself up off the floor. "I'm into it."

"Go pee, go pee!" Lucy commanded excitedly. "Hurry!" Aria laughed again.

"I'm going, I'm going!"

Lucy and Aria laid together intertwined on the couch, kissing and hugging, letting their hands wander. Aria's glasses were pushed up onto her head, and threatening to fall off. Without missing a beat, she removed them with one hand, folded them, and let them drop to the floor. The heat was rising between them, and they both could feel it. Lucy felt her heart race and she felt that familiar tingle of excitement between her legs. It had been a while since she'd had sex. And she was achingly eager for it.

Just as Lucy pressed forward and unbuttoned Aria's pants, signaling her intentions, the sound of a bolt unlocking echoed from the other room. They both heard it and swiftly pulled back from their embrace, eyes wide. The surprise drained from Lucy's face when she realized what it was.

"My Mom's home," she said with some of the greatest disappointment she'd ever felt.

They leaped from the couch and began to quickly straighten up. Lucy folded the blanket and tossed it on top of the couch, as Aria searched for her glasses and re-positioned them on her face. Lucy bent over to pick up a pillow from the floor as Aria buttoned her pants back, and when Aria saw Lucy bend, she reached back and gave Lucy's ass a firm slap.

"Eep!" intoned Lucy in surprise. Aria laughed.

Lucy righted herself and turned to wag a finger at Aria. But she couldn't suppress her smile.

Soon, the girls were back on the couch, with some space

between them, sipping cider once more. There was further commotion in the kitchen now, the sound of keys hitting the counter. They waited in silence, both trying to still their racing hearts.

"Hello?" said Jean's voice from the other room.

"In here," Lucy called back. Aria then leaned her lips in to Lucy's ear.

"I'm really wet for you," said Aria teasingly in a whisper. Lucy looked to her and admonished her with a slap on the knee. Aria laughed.

"Stop," said Lucy in a similar whisper. "I can't believe I'm thirty-five years old and I'm being walked in on by my..."

Jean entered the living room with a calm smile about her.

"Mom!" Lucy continued. "Welcome home. Did you have a good evening?"

"I did, dear," offered Jean, looking from Lucy to Aria and then back again. Jean once more looked to Aria and she smiled. "I'm Jean."

"Oh," replied Aria. "It's nice to meet you. I'm Aria."

"This is who I told you about, Mom," Lucy added. "From Fair Grounds. We went to the cider mill and got pumpkins yesterday."

"Ah, that's right," said Jean, nodding as it dawned on her. "I saw your work on the table. My, you two are up late."

"And you're home late," reflected Lucy. "I trust your night with Paul went swimmingly?"

"It did," Jean confirmed. "He's a very lovely man."

65

"Will we get to meet him someday?" asked Lucy, looking to Aria for backup. Aria smiled.

"We were talking about that," said Jean. "He's eager to meet you, too. I'm just... I want to take it slow."

"That's admirable," Aria butted in, offering a knowing look to Lucy. "Taking it slow is important in this fast-paced modern dating world."

"Thank you, Aria," said Jean. "I just want to make sure what we have is real. I don't want to bring my family into it if it's just another... thing."

"I don't think it's necessarily moving fast to be introduced to the man you're seeing, Mom," countered Lucy. "I'm just interested to see how you two interact, and if he's a good match for you."

"I appreciate that, dear," said Jean. "Perhaps the three of us will go out to eat together sometime soon. Then you can meet him in a neutral environment and let me know what you think."

"I think that's a good idea," said Lucy.

Aria smiled sheepishly, looking between Lucy and Jean now.

"It is actually getting late," said Aria. "I should probably be taking off." Lucy looked disappointed.

"All right," Lucy replied. "But I'll see you tomorrow at work."

"Of course," said Aria, now standing up from the couch. She turned to face Jean. "It was really great to meet you, Jean."

"You too, Aria," Jean agreed. They both smiled and

gently shook one another's hand. "Do you know your way out?"

"Yep, right around this way," said Aria, still smiling.

"I'll show you the way," said Jean cordially. "I'm heading that way to get ready for bed anyway."

Lucy watched this exchange with sustained disappointment. She really had it in her mind that Aria might stay over. But there was obviously some politics involved with that course as Lucy had her mother to contend with.

"Thank you," said Aria. "Goodnight, Lucy. I'll see you tomorrow, okay?"

"Yeah, okay," replied Lucy, trying to put on a smile. "Goodnight, Aria."

"Goodnight, dear," said Jean to Lucy with her kind smile. "Right this way, Aria."

"Thanks," Aria said. And then the two of them disappeared into the hallway, leaving Lucy sitting alone on the couch, feeling stupid and unfulfilled. She could tell the end of her night would be laying by herself in bed, imagining what might have been, with her hand shoved between her legs.

It felt all the more of a let down when she heard her Mom and Aria give one final exchange to each other and the shutting of the door. Lucy felt like a teenager again. It wasn't a great feeling.

CHAPTER 6

"Just head on down to the pickup counter," said Aria with a bright smile. "And Lucy will be right up with your latte."

"Thank you," said the customer, a woman in her fifties, mirroring Aria's smile. She packed her wallet back into her purse and walked on down the counter.

Lucy had gotten the hang of the espresso machine and filled the drink order with ease. As soon as she had the espresso locked and loaded, she deftly began steaming the milk in the stainless steel cup. The black coffee dripped in two streams into the mug below it, and as soon as it was finished Lucy retrieved the mug and poured the now-steamed milk into it. Mug in hand, she turned and approached the woman at the counter.

"Here you are, ma'am," Lucy offered. "Enjoy."

"Thank you very much," said the woman.

Back at the espresso machine, Lucy unhooked the

portafilter and knocked the spent puck of coffee grounds into the nearby bin. She rinsed off the portafilter and dried it, placing it delicately on top of the espresso machine. Then, when she was all finished, she wiped her hands dry with a clean towel she had set aside for exactly that purpose.

"Well, that was some rush," intoned Aria with a pleased sigh. She had appeared at Lucy's side without Lucy even realizing it.

"Yeah, it was," Lucy commiserated. "My pits are sweaty." Aria laughed.

"I don't smell nothing," teased Aria. Lucy grinned.

"That's very kind of you," said Lucy. "Hey, I forgot to tell you... you left your pumpkin at my house last night."

"Oh, I did that on purpose," said Aria. "That way, I have to come back to get it." They both laughed.

"Very sneaky of you," conferred Lucy. "I like it."

"It's just a shame that you didn't get to stick your hand into my guts last night, too," Aria joked. Lucy burst out laughing.

"I don't know whether to be grossed out by that or turned on," said Lucy.

"Why not both?" Aria replied, grinning and shrugging. She then pushed her black glasses up her nose.

"I really did have a good time last night with you, Aria," Lucy went on with a resolved seriousness. "These last few days with you, really. I mean, it's been great. I actually feel like I have a friend here in Madeira."

"You do!" beamed Aria. "You do have a friend."

"It feels like a win," said Lucy, still serious, looking wistful. "It's nice to have a win."

Aria maintained her smile, and she reached out and put her hand on Lucy's arm.

"We've only got an hour left before Wendy and Adam take over," Aria said. "I'm gonna go count our tips and see where we're at after that rush."

"Okay," said Lucy, taking a deep breath, steadying herself, and putting a smile back on.

"I was thinking that maybe after work," Aria continued. "You could come by my house and see where I live. Maybe meet my Dad."

"Yeah?" Lucy said, perking up a bit more. "I'd like that."

"Great," Aria surmised. "We'll stop by my place and see where the afternoon takes us. We'll see how many more wins we can get today." Lucy laughed happily and nodded.

"Thanks Aria," she said, her smile big and authentic. "Thank you."

ARIA'S HOUSE was large and ornate on the outside, though it was a kind of false ornateness that matched all the other houses in her subdivision. The front entry had a kitschy grandiosity to it, with a big wooden door and white columns that must have went up ten feet or more until they reached the overhang. Even though it was autumn and the leaves had been falling for a couple weeks, Aria's lawn was immaculate. As was every other home on the block.

"This is a nice place," mused Lucy, looking all over the house as she waited on the front steps for Aria to unlock the door.

"Thanks," said Aria. "But it's not really. It's just a McMansion. It's got a nice facade, but it was built on the cheap for what it is. This whole subdivision is a ruse."

Popping the door open, Aria stepped inside and Lucy eagerly followed behind her. The door closed.

Inside, they were met by a grand staircase and a chandelier hanging overhead. The floors were marble tile. Everything looked curated, like it was out of a magazine. It all looked like you weren't supposed to touch it.

"You must have a lot of space here to yourself," offered Lucy, following Aria's lead as they both removed their shoes. "It's just you and your parents, right?"

"Right," said Aria. "I do have a good amount of space upstairs. It's almost like my own wing." She laughed.

"I mean, that's pretty sweet," said Lucy. "My Mom's house is so small. We're always right on top of each other."

"Yeah, but your house has character," countered Aria. "It's older. It feels lived in and comfortable. This place..." she said, looking around at her own home. "I don't know. It doesn't feel like anything."

"So do your parents have their own wing upstairs?" asked Lucy. The girls were now walking down the hallway, entering into the kitchen.

"My Mom does," said Aria. "My Dad lives down here."

"Oh, right."

"He's pretty much always in that living room," Aria

confirmed, pointing to an adjoining room from which the subtle sounds of television could be heard. "And he has a bedroom over there." She pointed in another direction.

Lucy looked around the kitchen and took it all in. White shaker-style cabinetry, stainless steel appliances, a large apron sink. It was all so picture-perfect. She could feel a bit of jealousy welling up inside of her.

"This way," said Aria through her smile. "Let's meet my Dad."

When Lucy entered the sitting room behind Aria, her heart sank. The room itself was just as nice as the rest of the house, but that no longer did anything for Lucy. Instead, she just looked at Aria's Dad. He sat upright in a recliner with a blanket over his legs. He was old and looked frail and dour. His white hair was messed, and his glasses had slid down his nose. His eyes focused firmly on the television, a television with its volume turned up too loud. Aria approached her father, still smiling, and pushed his glasses up his nose.

"Hey Dad," said Aria joyfully. "I want you to meet my friend Lucy."

"Hi," Lucy offered meekly, stepping closer.

"His name is Theo," Aria told her. "Theodore Caspar."

"I mean, can he..." Lucy said, coming closer still. "Can he hear us?"

"Yeah," Aria replied, still smiling. "He just comes and goes."

"I see."

"He was a pilot in the Korean War," Aria admitted. "He never had good things to say about it. Then he was an engineer for the rest of his life for the auto companies in Detroit. He worked at all of the Big Three at one time or another. He kept getting poached, you know? He helped refine how seat belts were used in cars."

"What? Really?" Lucy said in amazement. "You're kidding."

"Nope."

"Wow," mused Lucy.

"He's got a history," said Aria, her enthusiasm beginning to fade. "I just feel so awful that this is how his story ends."

"Yeah," agreed Lucy. "Yeah. It's sad."

"He was always a good guy," continued Aria. "And I just feel like he deserves better than this. Slowly fading away in this ticky-tacky house. He was always so sharp. And this place feels so dull."

"He married later in life," Lucy computed, trying to make sense of it all. "Your Mom is a lot younger than him."

"My Mom is his second wife," said Aria. "My Dad's first wife died of cancer when she was in her late forties. They had kids. My step-siblings. They're cool. But I don't see them very much."

"Damn," Lucy said. "I had no idea."

"My Mom kind of took advantage of him," Aria confided in Lucy with a certain sadness. "She's kind of a bitch."

Lucy didn't know what to say. She just stood there and listened.

"But I love my Dad," confirmed Aria. "And I want to make sure he's taken care of."

Lucy watched Aria as she pushed her finger up underneath her glasses, wiping a tear away from her eye.

After a few moments of silence, Lucy spoke up.

"I'm sorry, Aria."

Aria looked to her, and she smiled weakly.

———

LUCY SAT on a love seat in Aria's room, flipping through a thick blue book that she had found sitting on the small coffee table in front of her. The book was strange to her. It talked about "public cases" and had poetry in it, but much of it made little sense. The prose sections, which also had a poetic side to them, talked of masters and students and there were mentions of Buddha and rivers and kings and other ideas that felt impenetrable to Lucy.

Aria's room itself was quite large. It had an attached bathroom, and just outside of the room was another room that Aria had appointed as her office. Indeed, this wing of the house felt removed from the others that Lucy had seen. And the entire area that Aria claimed for herself was bigger than Lucy's apartment back in New York City.

"I'm back," said Aria, slinking into the bedroom and offering a smile to Lucy. "Thanks for being patient."

"Oh yeah," replied Lucy. "No problem at all."

"I just had to make lunch for my Dad and clean the kitchen up a little bit," Aria offered. She approached Lucy and looked at the book in her hands. "That's the Blue Cliff Record." Lucy looked at the book's cover and smiled.

"Yep."

"It's a book of Zen Buddhist koans," said Aria.

"Like... what's the sound of one hand clapping?" Lucy asked.

"Um, well... sort of," Aria surmised. "I guess. But not really."

"I looked through it and I don't really get it," said Lucy, handing the book over to Aria. Aria received the book and opened it up herself.

"Well, see," she began. "There's a lead-in pointer to the koan—which is just a public case, kind of like a master talking to a student. The pointer is by master Yuan Wu. Then there's the case, a traditional Zen scripture record. Then Yuan Wu gives his notes about the text. Then there's some poetry by Hsueh Tou about the case, then more commentary by Yuan Wu about the verse and—"

"Okay," Lucy interrupted with a laugh. "I think I'm a bit lost. Give it to me more plainly." Aria smiled.

"A Zen master says, 'you're about to read about some presumably enlightened fools.' You read about them," said Aria. "Then you read the Zen master pontificate about it, often sarcastically. Then it's all done again with poetry." Lucy laughed again.

"Okay, got it," she said. "So are you a Buddhist?"

"Not really," Aria said. "I mean, no. I just think it's helpful to read." She dropped the book once more to the coffee table.

"Huh," mused Lucy, looking back toward the book.

"Did you search through any of my other things?" Aria

teasingly asked. "Did you look in my box of personal affects? Find my cash? Rifle through my underwear drawer?" Lucy laughed even bigger.

"No!" she protested. "I've been sitting here the entire time." Lucy smiled simply. "Really."

"Well, you can if you want," said Aria with a grin. Lucy just smiled and shook her head.

"I've got to say," Lucy went on. "This is a nice room. You've got an en suite bathroom. Big windows. So much space. Aria, you have a couch in your bedroom. This place is cush."

"I know," admitted Aria, looking a bit embarrassed by Lucy's assertions. "It's just a bit too much for me, that's all. I've been in the process of downsizing. I've got so much stuff accumulated throughout my life, and I just don't need any of it. Maybe that doesn't make sense. But it just feels right to me."

"I mean, I can help," Lucy offered happily. "Listen, when I came to terms with the fact that I had to leave New York, I got rid of what I had to, shoved the rest into storage, and came back here to Michigan with just a few bags. I downsized out of necessity."

"Maybe I do need a little help," Aria mused. She looked lost in thought for a moment but then shook it off with a smile. "What do you think your future looks like?"

"My future?" replied Lucy. "Um, well, I used to think I had a good grasp on my future but now I'm not so sure. I guess I just want to get my shit back together. Get a full-time job again. Get my own place again. The basics."

"Let's pretend you have all that," pushed Aria. "What then?"

"Hmm," intoned Lucy, staring off and letting the question sink in. She was transported back to her life in New York, the dreams she had been building on, her hopes for the future. The old ideas were still there, but they were distant and they were transparent, almost as though they were evaporating into the ether.

Aria patently waited with a pleasant look on her face. She gave Lucy the space she needed.

"Well," Lucy said, as she tried to put into words the images she saw. "I used to think about owning my own brownstone in Park Slope, near Prospect Park in Brooklyn. I would be an executive at my company, and money just would no longer be an issue. My kitchen would be immaculate. Big farmhouse sink, quartz counters, heated tile floor. One of those fancy professional ovens with the red knobs." She looked to Aria and smiled, making a bit of a silly face to convey that she knew how it all sounded. Aria offered her a knowing laugh.

"So... just stuff," said Aria. "Right? You just aspire to stuff?"

"Stuff?" repeated Lucy. "I don't know. I guess. Isn't that why we work so hard? To get nice stuff? I mean... right?"

"Maybe," said Aria in a tone indicating she might disagree. She paused. "But you know, I come from stuff. This house is full of fancy things. Or, well... in my opinion, pseudo-fancy. Style, but no substance. And I didn't even have to work for it myself."

"So maybe you take it for granted," countered Lucy. "Have you considered that?"

"That could be," Aria replied. "Or maybe I just know it's not the answer because I've lived it."

"Well, okay then," pushed Lucy. "Your turn. What do you see in your future?"

"Um," said Aria, pushing a strand of her blonde hair back behind her ear. "I'm going to be real with you for a minute here."

Aria's change in demeanor and tone suddenly caught Lucy off-guard.

"Yeah, okay," said Lucy in a mirrored seriousness. "Of course."

"I know that my Dad is going to die one day," offered Aria solemnly. "That's a given. And it could be at any time, really. He's sick, he's fading. I'm really just sticking around here for him because I can't trust that my Mom will take good enough care of him."

"Right," Lucy said, nodding slowly in knowing agreement.

"I have..." Aria began, giving herself a split second to weigh her words. "A trust fund. I have money waiting for me."

"I see."

"It's not a fortune," she clarified. "But it's substantial. And I actually don't get it until my Dad passes. He's the executor or manager or whatever of it, and we weren't able to get that changed before he went downhill. But I really didn't care. I didn't care to push it, you know?"

"Okay," said Lucy, following along Aria's story.

"I don't mind working at the coffee shop for my spending money," Aria continued. "I'm fine. But whatever," she said, putting her hand up and trying to get back on track. "When I think about the future, there's some sadness in it. But there's also a new hope. And I don't know what I want with that new hope, I just know that I need to get out of this house and figure out the path I'm meant to be on."

"I think you will," Lucy consoled with a warm smile. Reaching out, she took Aria's hand. Aria looked at it and smiled.

"I think so, too," replied Aria softly. She squeezed Lucy's hand. It felt good to confide in her. It felt good to have someone so close.

CHAPTER 7

*L*ucy and Jean sat opposite one another at the restaurant table. The table was rustic, made of reclaimed wood and industrial steel, and the restaurant mirrored this aesthetic. It was an upscale barbecue place and the table came complete with a small lazy susan of hot sauce. Both Lucy and Jean were dressed in nicer clothing, maybe a little too nice for a dinner that could be messy. In front of Lucy was a small cocktail, while Jean sipped on a water.

"He's late," confirmed Lucy, looking to the small watch on her wrist. She took a drink from her glass and winced slightly.

"He's one minute late," Jean clarified and shook her head. "Don't be so critical."

"This cocktail is a little too strong," Lucy said, playing off of her Mom's assertion. "If I wanted to drink straight liquor I would have just ordered a glass of bourbon."

"Hush."

"I don't know," Lucy continued with her tease. "This just isn't boding well for the guy."

Just then a man entered the front of the restaurant and approached the hostess. He was older, but looked good for his age, slim with shortly cropped white hair. He wore a dark gray suit and a white button-down shirt with no tie. Jean watched him with wide, bright eyes as he spoke to the hostess, who in turn pointed across the restaurant to where Jean and Lucy sat. The man's eyes moved in that same direction, and when Jean was sure he saw her, she smiled big and waved. The man got a look of affirmation, he thanked the hostess, and then he made his way over.

"No more negativity," chastised Jean, holding a finger up to Lucy. Lucy was about to protest, but she let her Mom have this one. Jean then straightened herself out, she stood up from her seat, and came around to the front of the table as her beau approached.

"Jean," he said simply with a growing smile. "I'm sorry I'm late. I hit some traffic on the way home from work." Leaning in, he and Jean hugged and he kissed her on the cheek.

"You're not late at all," Jean countered. "Don't you worry about it."

"Thank you," he said, beaming.

"Paul, I'd like you to meet my daughter," Jean said, moving her palm in Lucy's direction. "This is Lucy. Lucy, this is Paul Vonn."

"Paul, it's nice to meet you," Lucy replied, now standing

up. She reached out and shook Paul's hand. Lucy was polished in her greeting, far more professional than she had been acting only moments before. Meeting people like Paul had been part of Lucy's old job and she was a pro.

"It's nice to finally meet you as well, Lucy," Paul agreed. "Jean has told me so much about you."

"Just know that my mother has a tendency to downplay my accomplishments," said Lucy with a straight face. "I'm far better than she lets on." Paul grinned and nodded, as Jean made a confused face.

"And what is that supposed to mean?" Jean asked.

"She's just pulling your leg," Paul said, placing his hand on Jean's shoulder. "Let's sit."

The party of three took their seats. It was obvious to Lucy immediately that her Mom was quite infatuated by Paul. And Lucy felt her heart warmed by this realization. Prior to meeting Paul, when he was just an idea, Lucy had felt protective of Jean. She felt a little unnerved that Jean was moving on from her dead father, no matter how selfish and disrespectful that idea was. But even just with this primary introduction, Lucy could feel herself growing happy for her Mom. The woman deserved it, after all.

"So my Mom tells me you work for an auto company," said Lucy. "And you live here in Madeira?"

"Yes," Paul agreed. "Both are true. I'm an executive vice president in public relations. And I moved to Madeira about ten years ago."

"How's everything at your company?" asked Lucy carefully. "With this... economic fallout, I mean."

"We're actually doing fine," Paul offered up. "We learned a valuable lesson from the last recession. Our bailout was fully paid back and this time around we were much more conservative with our debt-to-income ratio, so we don't expect any great failures. We're using this time to adapt to the changing market."

"That's good to hear," replied Lucy, returning his smile.

"Paul is very good at his job," Jean interjected. "His company is maintaining a very good image this time around. No layoffs!"

"No layoffs," echoed Lucy. "That's admirable."

"We were prepared this time," Paul reiterated.

"Sadly, Lucy was laid off," Jean said. Lucy gave her a look.

"I'm sorry to hear that," Paul consoled, but Lucy was certain he already knew that about her. She was certain he knew that she had been in New York, that everything in her life had failed, and now she was living back at home with her mother.

"I've had better years," said Lucy glibly. Paul smiled and nodded. "I worked as an account manager for a marketing firm. I know that can translate to many other industries and opportunities."

"That's true," said Paul. "And now that you're back in Michigan, you would do well to consider automotive."

"Does everybody in southeast Michigan have some sort of job at least tangentially related to automotive?" Lucy quipped. Paul laughed.

"Perhaps," he agreed. "Still, I believe there's plenty of

opportunity here and you should consider it. Jean has told me, though, you plan to return to New York."

"That has been the plan," confirmed Lucy. She took a drink.

"It has been nice having you back home," Jean said. "You know how much I missed you when you were away."

"This feels like some sort of intervention," Lucy joked with a raised brow. "If I had a choice, I would certainly take any professional job, be it here or in New York, over working in a local coffee shop. It's really not up to me, at this point."

Lucy was beginning to feel a bit cornered, as though this were some kind of setup. She stewed on the idea for a moment, stirring her drink, wondering what the motive was. Rather than wallow in her growing negative thoughts, Lucy mustered up the resolve to push through. She took a deep breath and forged a new smile on her face.

"Anyway," she said in conclusion of that line of conversation. "Paul, why don't you tell me a little more about yourself? You seem to know a lot about me. Let's hear something new about you?"

———

THAT NIGHT LUCY laid alone in her bed, staring up at the ceiling, lost in thought. She had been back home for a few months now and it still wasn't any more comfortable. It still felt foreign, even though she had grown up in this room. It didn't feel like her life. It felt like a long, lucid nightmare. She hated looking up at that popcorn ceiling in her small room, trying to force herself to sleep. It felt like she would never get out of this rut. When she was by herself at night, it was hard to avoid thinking that this was her new normal.

Since moving back to Madeira and experiencing this major life change, Lucy had developed some new anxiety. The running helped, and the job at the coffee shop helped some as well, but what helped the most was spending time with Aria. It felt like something was happening there, and in the past—when she was living her previous life as a successful adult—Lucy would have pursued the girl with greater fervor. But there was a new self-consciousness now that she was having a rough time dealing with. And how do you chase romance with someone when neither of you have your own private space?

This didn't feel like her life. This didn't feel like her reality. Why was she here?

Lucy didn't sleep very well that night, and in the morning she was groggy and sluggish. She stumbled out of bed and slipped into some lounge pants. Taking a deep breath, she sauntered over to the full-length mirror on the opposite side of the room. Lucy lifted her shirt up and took a look at her belly. She couldn't quite tell if she was making any progress. Her love handles did look a bit smaller. Turning side to side, Lucy inspected herself once more. Then she dropped the hem of her shirt, turned from the mirror, and left the room.

When she entered the kitchen, Jean was there, already dressed for the day and sorting through a bundle of mail. She raised a mug of coffee to her lips and took a drink. As she lowered it back to the counter, she spotted Lucy and she smiled.

"Good morning, sleepyhead," said Jean.

"Morning," offered Lucy casually, wandering over to the coffee pot to pour a mug of her own.

"Did you sleep well?"

"I did not," replied Lucy. She took a drink and tasted the ratio of her mix. She added more cream.

"I'm sorry, dear," Jean consoled. "Perhaps staying up late and watching reality television isn't the way to a good night's rest."

Lucy looked at her mother and rolled her eyes. Jean smirked.

"Thank you for coming out with Paul and I last night," Jean continued on. "I'm really happy that you finally were able to meet him."

"Yeah, no problem," Lucy responded, taking another sip of coffee. "He's fine. You have my blessing."

"That's good to hear," said Jean. "Listen..."

Lucy raised an eyebrow.

"Paul has invited me away for the weekend," Jean went on cautiously. "He has a home up on Torch Lake in Northern Michigan. The colors are beautiful up there right now."

"All right..." Lucy said slowly.

"And I've decided to go," said Jean. "I wanted you to meet him before I did anything like this. Do you feel all right about it? Do you think I should go?"

"Mom, I think you're a grown woman who can make

her own choices," said Lucy. "You're dating a guy, that's great, I'm happy for you. Go on your trip."

"It doesn't upset you or anything..." Jean asked. "That I'm seeing somebody?"

"Why would it?"

"Because of your father," said Jean.

"Dad... died," Lucy said matter-of-factly. "I mean, not to be coarse about it or anything, but he's gone."

"I know, dear."

"You deserve to be happy, Mom," said Lucy. "Please. Allow yourself to be happy."

Jean smiled and slowly nodded. Then she sighed and took a sip of coffee. The two were silent for a few moments.

"So this coming weekend?"

"That's right," said Jean.

"I'll hold down the fort," offered Lucy. "And don't worry, I won't have any parties." She smiled and winked. Jean chuckled.

"I wouldn't expect you to," she said.

"Besides," said Lucy. "I really don't even know anyone to invite over."

LUCY CAME JOGGING around the corner to a new block, her cheeks rosy, her dark brown ponytail bouncing. The air was crisp and it felt good in her lungs, her breathing steady and focused as she put one foot in front of the other. A remnant from her previous life, Lucy's activewear made her look like she had money, the logos on the clothing conveying their high cost. Now that her life had changed, she felt silly about spending that kind of money on workout clothes. But at the same time, they gave her a certain confidence when she was out running like this. They made her feel as though this was what she was supposed to be doing.

As she bounded down the block, Lucy noticed a sign in her path on the sidewalk. Upon getting closer, the sign became legible and it informed Lucy that there was an open house happening. She turned her head as she approached and saw a second sign in the front yard of the home, a sign that advertised the house being for sale by Phyllis Caspar. Lucy slowed her gait and then she stopped. She was curious. Changing her plans, Lucy walked up the pathway to the house, she opened the door, and she went inside.

The house was an older craftsman style home, on the smaller side, with a staircase to the right as soon as she came in. The floors underfoot were original wood, obviously refinished. There were decorative items and furniture in the house, but it was all staged. The house did not look lived in, it was merely on display.

Lucy carefully stepped inside further and looked around the house, absorbing it all. Everything was quiet apart from the occasional creaking sound of a floorboard below. Then she heard the sound of a woman's voice coming from the other room. Lucy paused and braced herself.

From the kitchen entryway came a woman dressed in a tan pantsuit. Her blonde hair was short and styled, her demeanor was serious. She held a phone up to her ear, and spoke into it. The woman looked very familiar to Lucy. She looked a lot like Aria.

"Yes, I believe we should increase our offer by ten thousand," said Phyllis. "You may not get another chance like this. People are swooping in with cash offers and sellers are taking those offers because it's a sure thing."

Phyllis paused when she saw Lucy standing there, and then she smiled at her and held up a single finger.

"That's great to hear," continued Phyllis. "I'll submit the offer in just another hour or so. Thank you, Dan and Kayla. I will report back as soon as I have news. Yes, you're welcome. Goodbye."

Phyllis brought her phone down from her ear and ended the call. Then she looked at Lucy once again and maintained her polished smile.

"Well, hello there," said Phyllis. "You're here for the open house."

"I saw the sign outside," replied Lucy. "And I thought I'd stop in."

"Are you in the market for a new home?"

"I am," Lucy lied.

"Splendid!" beamed Phyllis. "Well, welcome. My name is Phyllis Caspar and I am the seller's agent for this home. I have flyers right over here with all the particulars." As she said this, Phyllis waltzed over to a small table and retrieved a sheet of paper. In almost the same motion, she approached Lucy and handed it over.

"Thank you," said Lucy, accepting it.

"I think you'll find the price quite competitive,"

continued Phyllis, watching as Lucy looked over the sheet. "Is it just you searching for a home, or..."

"It's just me," replied Lucy. She looked up from the flyer and smiled.

"That's wonderful," Phyllis went on with a positive lilt in her voice. "A powerful woman doing it on her own. I can tell you're successful from your clothing. I'm assuming you already own your home here in Madeira, if you're out for a run around the block. If you haven't already engaged a real estate agent, I would be happy to assist you. My card is stapled there to the sheet." Phyllis pointed.

"Thank you," Lucy said once again. "I actually misspoke. It's not just me. Currently I have my younger sister living with me. She's fallen on hard times, what with this economic downturn and all. Would this home have enough space for the both of us to have our own separate living areas?"

"I suppose that depends on your needs," conferred Phyllis. "This being an older home, despite the recent remodel, there is only one shower and it is upstairs. So if you put your sister in the downstairs bedroom here, she would have to go upstairs to shower."

"I see," said Lucy, looking down into the informational flyer in her hands. "I'm not sure that will work. My sister is twenty-nine and she has her own needs, you know? I'm not sure we could share a bathroom like that."

"Oh yes, I understand," Phyllis replied. "My daughter is the same age and still lives at home. Fortunately, we have a rather large house and she's off in her own space. I couldn't imagine having to share bathroom space with her. I'm hoping one day she'll fly off on her own, but sadly that day will not be today."

"It's a tough time out there," Lucy said. "It might be difficult for your daughter to move out when the job market has dried up. That's sort of the issue my sister is having."

"My daughter is fine," offered Phyllis. "She could afford her own place if she wanted. Instead, she intends to leach off me and my husband until—"

Phyllis paused. Then she composed herself and smiled.

"I'm sorry," she said. "This is neither here nor there. To get back to your question, I'm not certain this home would would currently work for your situation. But if you were willing to lose a little space on the first floor, a shower could be installed in the bathroom here. I think you'd be looking at another fifteen thousand to rehab the first floor bathroom, which wouldn't be a bad idea. It would definitely add greater value to the home."

"Thank you," said Lucy. "I should actually get back to my run. But I'll hang on to this flyer."

"And my card," Phyllis commanded. "When you're interested in talking about selling your current home, please don't hesitate to give me a call."

"I will do that," Lucy replied with a knowing smile. "Thank you, Phyllis."

"You're more than welcome... I didn't catch your name, sweetie."

"Lucille," said Lucy, mirroring Phyllis' smile.

"Lovely name," Phyllis complimented. "You're welcome, Lucille."

After they both offered their goodbyes, Lucy turned from Phyllis and exited the house the same way she had entered. She took a deep breath and shook her head as she returned the chilly air outside. There was a nagging guilt in her mind from what she had done. Perhaps it was a step too far to speak with Aria's mother without her knowing. Their relationship was surely complicated. But Lucy had just been too curious. And Aria's summary of her mother was true. Phyllis was kind of a bitch.

Lucy wrestled with whether or not she would tell Aria what she had done. Surely, it wasn't too invasive. And she was certain that Aria would probably just roll her eyes and laugh at the dig her mother took at her. But Lucy's relation-ship—or whatever it was—with Aria was still new, and she didn't want to do anything to jeopardize that. If she had overstepped her bounds, it would probably be better to err on the side of caution and keep it to herself for now.

Picking up speed, Lucy regained her steady gait and felt her heart rate ramp up once more. Her eyes focused on the road ahead of her, and a bead of sweat rolled down her temple. In that moment, she felt strong.

CHAPTER 8

*E*ven though she was dressed down and casual, Lucy took some time to get ready. She penciled in her eyebrows and applied some mascara for a little extra eyelash volume. She carefully combed her hair back and wove it into a braid. Dressed in some flowing hemp pants and a chunky sweater, Lucy looked as though she were ready to lounge but it was a perfectly manicured look that had taken effort. After going through some bouts of self-consciousness, she finally took a look at herself in the bathroom mirror and smiled with satisfaction.

With Jean gone for the weekend, Lucy had the house to herself and the freedom she felt was explosive. It felt like a win in a sea of losses. This had been such a tumultuous year, it had all knocked Lucy down a notch, but the liberation she felt from her mother's getaway trip gave her a revitalized sense of agency. In a weird way, it was comforting. It gave Lucy hope that everything was going to be okay.

She curled up on the couch with the television on, trying to wait patiently but feeling impatient all the same. Lucy could hardly focus on whatever show it was she had put on. Instead, her thoughts hovered around her impending guest. Her heart raced and she hardly knew what to expect. Lately, all she could think about was Aria, to the neglect of other things in her life. It had been a few days since she'd even looked for jobs. She told herself she'd redouble her efforts on Monday. But it almost felt like it didn't matter.

When the doorbell finally rang, Lucy was spooked and she shivered. Then she jumped up off the couch and quickly scooted to the front door with an excited smile on her face, a smile that bordered on silly. Without hesitation, she yanked the door open.

Standing out on the porch was a smiling Aria. She was bundled up in a sherpa-lined canvas coat and a knit cap. In the streetlights behind her, the smallest flurries of snow could be seen. Aria shrugged happily and lifted her palms.

"Aria!" called Lucy in an almost sing-songy voice.

"Lucy!" replied Aria in refrain.

The girls hugged tightly, and then Aria came inside. A comfortable warmth hit them both.

Although they hadn't spoken about what was happening between them, it would be obvious to any outside observer. Their interactions had all grown much more flirty, and they texted each other daily. When they worked together at Fair Grounds, they were happily handsy with one another, conveying a sense of intimacy and affection. For Lucy, whatever it was that was happening with Aria had become her new focus without her quite realizing it. And when she finally did realize it, that night with the house to herself, she truly felt happy. She felt like things were going her way.

They talked and drank tea, animated in their conversation. The television had been turned off long ago, as it was unnecessary. As the night went on, the space between them diminished. They were sitting eagerly against one another, to the point where Aria was absently petting Lucy's leg. They both knew where this was headed, but it was almost like a game to see who would break first. Lucy could feel her heart thumping hard and the anticipation was killing her. Feeling like she might drop her mug of tea, Lucy turned slightly to put it down on the table next to the couch, and when she turned back she saw a smiling Aria push her glasses up on top of her head.

Lucy melted when their lips met, and immediately the two showed each other just how handsy they could be. While their kissing was slow and meditative, passionate and focused, Lucy buzzed excitedly as Aria's hand moved down her side and pushed to her inner thigh. Feeling Aria squeeze her thigh was the kind of intimacy that Lucy had craved for such a long time. She needed it. She required it. Lucy was eager, and as Aria's hand moved closer to her heat, Lucy herself let her hands explore her new lover. It had been a while since she grabbed a tit and squeezed. It was a feeling she'd missed.

When Aria pressed her hand between Lucy's legs, all Lucy could do was moan softly into Aria's mouth. Nothing else mattered but this moment. Her worries and cares had dissolved into nothingness. They were replaced by an aching desire, a carnal lust that had been absent for so long. Lucy throbbed with anticipation.

So when Aria stood up from the couch and began to lead the charge, Lucy went along with whatever she wanted. She watched as Aria undid the tie of Lucy's hemp pants, and pulled them down her legs, leaving Lucy in just her chunky sweater and her nicest purple lacy panties. It must have been obvious how orchestrated Lucy was for this evening, but now Lucy was simply eager to take it all off. With a devious look of lust on her face, Aria tugged at Lucy's underwear and before Lucy knew it, those too were being pulled down her legs and yanked off her feet.

Now, in just that over-sized sweater, feet on the couch, knees up and her legs wide, Lucy watched intently as Aria buried her face between her thighs and explored her with her tongue. She felt drunk, despite not having a drop of alcohol all evening. Aria's blonde hair was pushed behind her ears, her dark glasses still rested on top of her head, she had undressed down to her bra, and her eyes were closed as she slowly and adeptly ate Lucy out.

"That's so good," Lucy said in a near whisper. She closed her eyes for a moment, focusing on the pleasure, but Lucy couldn't stay blind for long. She wanted to watch. As she opened her eyes back up to return her gaze to her pleasure, Lucy watched as Aria planted a deep, full, wet kiss on her clit.

Lucy was sweating, and she longed to pull that sweater up over her head and toss it away, but there was no opportunity. Instead she just grew hotter and endured, putting her hands on her knees and pulling at her legs, as though she could spread them further open. Aria's head was turned to one side, her tongue lapping at Lucy's clit, and she firmly and slowly pressed two fingers inside of Lucy, only to pull them out and then push them in again.

A feeling of light-headedness overtook Lucy, and she relaxed her neck, dropping her head back onto the couch. She gave herself over to the sex and she felt a familiar twinkling her in her toes. It was when Aria pursed her lips against Lucy's clit and kissed it with a firm suck that Lucy began to quiver. Her pussy squeezed onto Aria's fingers, and her thighs quaked. Lucy felt tremors throughout her body. Her mouth was agape and groans of fulfillment emanated from it. Lucy felt high.

Lucy opened her eyes and looked downward once she felt Aria's attentions cease. She selfishly craved more, the image of Aria wiping the wetness from her mouth with the back of her hand filled her with a greater sense of admiration and gratitude. Lucy knew it was her turn.

Aria caught her looking, and she smiled alluringly. Then she blew Lucy a kiss. Lucy was still breathing heavily and happily, and all she could do was put on a dumb smile. Then Aria laughed softly.

"You made a mess," Aria teased. With a single finger, she traced down through Lucy's slit, accumulating some of the tacky wetness on her finger.

"Yeah, I'm totally wet right now," replied Lucy between breaths.

"No, I mean you soaked the couch," said Aria. She laughed once more.

"What? Really?" Lucy asked with a sudden sense of worry. "Damn it."

"Next time we'll put a towel down," proposed Aria with a grin. She delicately ran her fingers up and down Lucy's pussy. Her eyes lingered on it for a moment, while her grin remained.

"Screw it," said Lucy. "I'll just clean it tomorrow."

"You're cute," said Aria. But Lucy wasn't sure if Aria was referring to her worry over the mess or her pussy. She put her arm over her eyes and absorbed a sudden wave of self-consciousness.

"I try too hard," Lucy said, almost out of nowhere.

"What? No," protested Aria. "Are you talking about this?" When she said 'this,' Aria again moved her fingers along Lucy's pussy. The flesh of her lips was smooth and waxed, while her bush above was neatly trimmed. Lucy had obviously prepared herself for the possibilities of the evening.

"Yes," said Lucy, still feeling slight embarrassment.

"I told you, I think it's cute," repeated Aria. "I love it. It makes me happy to know you were thinking of me when you... prepared." Aria couldn't help but grin.

Lucy dropped her arm from where it rested on her face and wore a silly smile. She felt vulnerable sitting there, legs still spread, being examined and evaluated by the beautiful Aria, but that vulnerability was comforting. Lucy had never felt closer to Aria.

"Listen," said Aria. "Let's not talk about this anymore. It's my turn and I don't like to be kept waiting."

With this, Aria stood up from her perch between Lucy's legs. She wore only her jeans and a small white bra. Lucy watched as Aria unbuttoned her jeans, slid them down her legs, and stepped out of them. She stood there for a moment with a teasing look on her face, pushing a single finger from each hand into either side of her black underwear. Aria stretched the band out and then pushed the fabric down over her hips. After the underwear got midway down her thighs, they simple fell to her ankles and Aria stepped out of them. Her blonde bush matched her hair, and when she caught Lucy looking at her middle, Aria ran her fingers over her curly pubes.

"I'm not as well-groomed as you," Aria quipped with a laugh. Lucy smiled wide, feeling her excitement build once again.

Finally, Aria reached behind her back and unclasped her bra. Taking the straps off her shoulder and removing the cups, Aria revealed her tits. They were small, but buoyant. Her areolas were small and her nipples were big, stiff, each sticking out from her breasts about half an inch. Lucy couldn't help but stare. She had spent so many nights imagining what Aria looked like naked, and now she was right in front of her.

"They're always hard," Aria mused, flicking her finger at one of her nipples. "If I don't wear a padded bra..." She laughed and shook her head.

Lucy jumped up from the couch, still in just her sweater,

which hung down to about her upper thigh. Reaching out, she grabbed Aria by the hand and tugged at her, pulling her in the direction of her bedroom. Aria laughed and eagerly followed. As they raced, Aria's glasses feel from her head and tumbled down to the carpet. She broke away from Lucy for that moment, retraced a few steps back, and leaned down to pick them back up.

In that moment, Lucy caught the slightest glimpse of Aria's pussy from her backside. It was almost as though Aria had bent down like that on purpose. And when Aria looked back at Lucy, still bent down, now with her glasses back on her face, she grinned wildly. Lucy could hardly contain her reemerging arousal. This felt like the best night of her life.

WHEN LUCY OPENED her eyes the next morning, the first thing she saw was the popcorn ceiling above her bed. And then, looking to her side, the next thing she saw was Aria sharing her bed with her. How they had slept together in that bed in comfort was a mystery to Lucy. It was such a small mattress, and the only way they fit was pressed up against each other. Lucy could feel her damp, sweaty skin where it touched Aria under the covers. It warmed her heart to be so close to Aria.

The clock next to the bed informed Lucy that it was just after eight in the morning. She briefly considered closing her eyes once more and attempting to grab a bit more sleep. The last time she remembered looking at that clock was around three, after coming up from between Aria's legs to watch her face as she orgasmed. She was still tired from their night of taking turns pleasuring one another, and another few hours of sleep could be in order.

But as Lucy stirred, so did Aria. With a cute little groan of wakefulness, Aria turned over in bed so that they now faced each other. Her blue eyes opened groggily and a tired smile moved over Aria's lips.

"Morning," Aria said blithely.

"Hi," whispered Lucy happily.

The girls kissed. And then they kissed again. Soon, their hands were exploring one another with eager excitement, almost as though their sleeping had been but a minor break in the middle of their lovemaking. But feeling something caught in her lip, Lucy pulled back slightly and brought her hand to her mouth. Aria watched with curiosity, a small grin coming to her own lips as Lucy crossed her eyes slightly, watching her own hand. Lucy then took hold of a single hair and pulled it. She smiled.

"It's one of yours," Lucy said, passing the thin blonde hair over to Aria. Aria took it and laughed.

A bit later, Aria sat at a barstool pushed up to the counter in Lucy's kitchen. She sipped on a mug of coffee, feeling cozy and warm in a large fleece sweater that she had plucked from Lucy's closet. Lucy meanwhile was making breakfast. In a bowl, she mashed up an avocado, adding in some salt and pepper, and a few cherry tomatoes that she had quartered. Aria watched her with a song in her heart and a casual smile on her face. Aria's eyes remained focused on Lucy as she spread the avocado onto a piece of toasted sourdough bread.

With two plates in hand, Lucy approached the side of the counter where Aria sat and she set the plates down, one in front of Aria and one in front of herself. Aria looked down at the plate hungrily.

"Mmm!" Aria intoned. "This looks perfect."

"Do you need any more coffee?" asked Lucy as she poured some coffee into her own mug from the french press.

"No, I'm good," replied Aria. "Thank you so much. I don't remember the last time someone made breakfast for me."

"What? Really?" said Lucy. Then she remembered Aria's situation, and suddenly felt guilt for her words.

"Yeah, you know..." offered Aria. "I do most of the cooking at home, and I'm a server at work. So..."

Aria smiled and shrugged. Then she picked up her piece of avocado toast and took a big bite. Grinning and chewing, she wiped at the corner of her mouth to remove an errant smudge of avocado.

"I'm sorry," said Lucy. "I shouldn't have been so incredulous. I forgot, that's all."

"Oh no, no!" Aria replied quickly, holding her palm up like she was wiping the slate clean. "You're fine. This is amazing," she said, returning the conversation back to the food.

"Thanks," said Lucy. She took her own bite and chewed with a smile.

"Can I be real with you for a minute?" Aria asked. Lucy let out a small nervous laugh.

"Real with me?" she volleyed back. "Of course you can be real with me."

"Okay," Aria said. She put her toast down and wiped her hands on a napkin. Then she sat up straight on the stool.

Lucy raised an eyebrow, wondering what could possibly come out of Aria's mouth next.

"You know, I was really nervous about last night," Aria finally admitted. "I knew when I was coming over here that we'd probably... sleep together. And I just don't have a lot of experience."

"Well, you know your way around a vagina pretty well," quipped Lucy. Aria laughed.

"I mean, I have one... so..." Aria replied. They both smiled. "No, I just mean to say... I didn't really have a sex with another girl until I was in college. And once I moved back home, here in Madeira, there just hasn't been a lot of opportunity to meet a girlfriend. Between taking care of my Dad and working, it just never came together for me."

"That's okay," Lucy confirmed. "Seriously, you have nothing to be nervous about. The sex was great."

"It's been a long time for me," Aria continued. "Like I said, I slept with a few girls back in college. But since then, over the last half dozen years or so, I've only had sex with one girl. And that was a really short relationship. I guess it's just hard because I'm also not really out to my parents yet."

"Oh," said Lucy, finally beginning to understand where

this was going. More of the picture of Aria was coming together.

"As wonderful as my Dad was... is..." began Aria. "Neither he or my Mom are very accepting of... being gay. It's hard, and it gives me a lot of anxiety. People are complicated."

"People certainly are complicated."

"I'm sorry," said Aria solemnly, looking away for a moment.

"No, listen," said Lucy, reaching her hand across the counter and placing it on Aria's. "It's okay. I totally understand. And I don't want you to be anxious about anything around me. Like I said, you were great. I loved it. And I want to do it again."

Aria looked back to Lucy and slowly smiled.

"I want to do it again, too," Aria agreed.

"Then it's settled," Lucy said, holding her mug up toward Aria. "We'll be having sex again."

Aria laughed and held her own mug up, tapping it on Lucy's. They both then took a drink of coffee. Something unique was brewing between them. It was a palpable feeling to both of them.

CHAPTER 9

Some time had passed, and dressed in a blue and gray wool coat, Lucy sauntered up the walkway to her house while snow fell around her. It was a beautiful scene, and after a tiring morning slinging lattes it was a revitalizing treat. Lucy had worked with Adam that morning, and while he was fine to work next to, she always wished it could be Aria by her side. Her mind danced around thoughts of Aria and her sweet face as Lucy unlocked the front door and stepped into the warmth of the house.

As Lucy entered, she immediately spotted her Mom, who had a coat on herself. Jean hoisted her purse up onto her shoulder and then she saw Lucy.

"Hello there, dear," said Jean with a smile. "I was just about to head out."

"Oh?" offered Lucy. She removed her own bag and set it on a table near the door. Then she took her coat off and moved to hang it on a coat rack.

"I have to run some errands," said Jeans. "To the bank and the grocery store. Is there anything you need?"

"Nope, I'm good," Lucy said, giving her Mom a smile.

"Good," replied Jean. "Did you have a nice morning at work?"

"It was okay," Lucy conferred with a shrug and flat lips.

"That reminds me," Jean began. "Paul told me he thinks there could be a position in his department opening up that you would be a nice fit for. He said they were planning on doing an internal hire, but it didn't work out right so now they're going to start looking for an outside candidate."

"I don't know about that, Mom," replied Lucy skeptically. "I think that's weird. Me working for the guy you're dating. What if something happens and you break up? Now he's going to take it out on me at work. I'm not sure it's a good idea."

"You're overthinking this, dear," Jean sniped back. "Besides, both Paul and I are adults and if the relationship doesn't work out we'll both be perfectly mature about it."

"I don't think I'm overthinking it," Lucy countered. "I've personally seen that kind of thing happen at work. A very similar situation. A manager's girlfriend got a friend of hers in, the manager and his girlfriend broke up, and this manager gave the girl a bunch of shit clients that nobody wanted. I would have hated to be that girl."

"Not everybody holds such grudges," said Jean. "All I'm asking you to do is to consider it. If you're interested, I'll let Paul know and you can go from there."

"Mom, I just don't—"

"Please," Jean pleaded. "Just consider it. Okay?"

Lucy paused. She took a breath and then she nodded in agreement.

"I'll consider it."

"Thank you," said Jean. She reapplied her smile. "Now I'm off. Are you sure there's nothing you need at the store?"

"I'm sure," said Lucy. "Thank you."

"I'll return shortly," Jean confirmed. "Text me if you can think of anything."

"I will."

"Goodbye, dear."

Jean offered one more smile before stepping past Lucy and exiting through the front door.

Lucy stood there in the entryway for a few moments and meditated on what Jean had said. It wasn't an ideal situation, of course, to work for her mother's boyfriend. But getting a job at one of the auto companies could be a huge career move for Lucy. It could be the start of something great. It wasn't exactly what she was after, but she was beginning to feel desperate. Her longing to move back to New York was outweighed by her need to get herself back into an office job.

Stepping to a window, Lucy stared outside and watched the falling snow. It was just now beginning to cover the grass, though the sidewalk out front was still bare. The concrete looked darker and damp. It was actually a pretty nice day out, the sun occasionally peeking through the clouds, the temperature just low enough that it could snow, very little wind. The thought struck Lucy that she should keep up her routine and go for a run.

In her room, Lucy peeled out of her work clothes and tossed them into her hamper. She placed her bra over the back of a chair. Standing in just her underwear, she approached the full-length mirror and looked herself over. She could tell she was making progress. Turning to the side, she scoped herself out further. She pinched at one of her love handles. It would never go away, and nor did she want it to. But she was feeling confident and happy that her body was returning to what it once had been. She was feeling much more comfortable in her own skin.

The stresses of life in New York and her demanding job had made it difficult to take care of herself. But with this break in life that had been handed to her, she was starting to practice some better self-care. And it was working. She couldn't stop now. She had to press on.

Lucy opened up her dresser and began to pull out her running gear. She maneuvered into some thicker winter workout tights. She wove herself into her sports bra. Then came a long-sleeve shirt and a stretchy hoodie on top of that. Socks and shoes and suddenly she was ready to go. In her former life, after coming home from work, she might have just poured herself a glass of wine and plopped down in front of the television. But now that she got off work in the early afternoon, there was still plenty of daylight left for her to get outside and get her heart racing.

Back in the entryway of the house, Lucy grabbed at her foot and stretched her leg, pulling her heel to her butt. She held the stretch for a moment, and then she did the other leg. This wasn't so bad. Her life was really okay. She was getting into shape, she was seeing somebody, and it was starting to make her feel like things were falling into place. Maybe she would have her Mom connect her with Paul. Maybe this was how it was supposed to work out.

Lucy opened the door and stepped out into the cold air outside. It was certainly brisk. The chill filled her lungs as she inhaled, and then exhaled a puff of steam. She did it again to ready herself, and then she took off. She jogged steadily down the walkway until she reached the sidewalk, then she turned left and went for it. The snow fell all around her, and Lucy wore a smile as she ran. It was the perfect day for it.

THE NEXT DAY, bundled up tightly in her winter coat, Aria walked from the front door of her house to her car, trudging through the snow in her tall boots. The driveway needed to be plowed, as the previous night's snowfall had been the biggest of the season yet. Aria started her car up to get the heat going, and she yanked a large blue snow brush from her backseat. She proceeded to clean off her windshield and windows, easily knocking the fluffy white precipitation from the glass.

It was nearing one in the afternoon, and although Aria wasn't yet late for work, she was getting close to the point where she could be late. Feeling a bit annoyed, Aria quickly finished cleaning the snow from her car. She had given her Dad lunch already, but her Mom was supposed to be home already to take over caring for him. In the last week, Aria's father had taken a turn and was requiring even more help than he had been. Phyllis was not rising to the task.

And now, feeling a growing sense of anger, Aria was having to leave her Dad all alone and head in to work. It was far from ideal, but there was nothing she could do.

Just as Aria was tossing her snow brush back into the backseat, slamming the door behind it, a white SUV pulled up into the driveway next to her. Although a sense of relief washed over Aria, she was still annoyed. Her mother had really cut it close.

"I was beginning to think you totally forgot," sniped Aria as soon as her Mom got out of the car.

"I didn't forget," Phyllis lobbed back. "I told you I'd arrived around one."

"I have to be to work by one," said Aria with anger. "I told you twelve thirty."

"Well, I'm here," said Phyllis. "Stop worrying about it and go."

"We both need to pull more weight around here if we're going to be able to take care of him," Aria chastised. "I feel like I'm already doing all that I can."

"Then maybe it's time we get him some professional care," Phyllis replied. "I told you that I've looked into nursing homes and I have found a few great candidates."

"I'm not having this discussion again right now," said Aria. "I'm going to work."

"Have a wonderful day," Phyllis offered with wide, sarcastic eyes.

Aria shook her head. She opened the door of her car, slid inside, and prepared to take off. Before she left, however, she watched her Mom casually trot up to the house like nothing really mattered. It made Aria see red.

By the time she was on the road, Aria was already calming down. She knew who her mother was and she knew how the woman acted. There would be no changes until her father's time came, and even then Phyllis would continue on in her ways. It didn't make any sense for Aria to get so worked up over her mother's actions. She just had to continue living with them for now.

The roads had been plowed and salted, but the drive was still a bit slick and snow was starting to fall heavier still. By the time Aria parked and began her walk to the coffee shop on Main Street, the snow was really coming down. Big, fluffy flakes dancing down from the heavens. One flitted down and landed directly behind Aria's glasses, wetting her eye. She pushed her hand up underneath her glasses to wipe the water away as she pulled the coffee shop door open with the other.

The coffee shop was warm and cozy, but it was much emptier than Aria thought it would be at this time of day. There were only three customers sitting around, and two of them looked as though they were readying themselves to leave. Aria sauntered up to the counter where Wendy stood. Wendy smiled as she saw Aria approach.

"What's the deal?" Aria asked. "Where is everybody?"

"Didn't you see the weather?" replied Wendy. "Another big snow storm is coming. We're supposed to get even more than we did overnight. I think people are hunkering down."

"Huh," mused Aria, looking around the cafe once more. "Are we going to stay open for our usual hours?"

"As of now, yeah," Wendy said. "But give me a call if it gets really bad and nobody's coming in."

"Lucy's coming in at two, right?"

"Yeah," said Wendy. "We'll try to stay open at least until six. Let's just see how the night goes."

"All right," confirmed Aria. She looked out the front window and the snow had become a whiteout. After a moment of watching it, lost in thought, Aria removed her coat and walked away from the counter and to the backroom.

THE SNOW DID NOT STOP all afternoon. And the only customers they got were people who had stopped in for a to-go cup of coffee on their way home from work. By five o'clock the sun was setting and the storm was raging. It was actually quite a beautiful sight, the snow falling heavy in the glowing streetlights. Lucy and Aria sat together at a table, each with a mug of coffee. They slowly sipped and watched the snowfall.

"Think we're going to get trapped here?" Lucy asked absently, eyes focused on the snow. There was a quiet, wistful feeling hovering in the air of the cafe. A nondescript melancholy.

"That would be something," replied Aria. "We'd be eating muffins for dinner."

"I think we're out of muffins."

"Cheesecake, then."

"That would not be a bad dinner," quipped Lucy. Aria smiled.

"I didn't tell you..." Aria began, opening up. "My Dad got worse this week. It's been rough."

"I'm sorry, babe," Lucy offered with empathetic eyes. She reached across the table and put her hand on Aria's.

"It's okay," Aria said. "It's just been emotional for me. On Thanksgiving, it seemed like he was actually getting better. A few weeks later, this. I didn't want you to think I had been avoiding you or anything. I've just been busy and stressed."

"I understand," said Lucy. She gave Aria a small smile. "I've been feeling kind of down this week, anyway. Maybe it's just the season. There's something about the beginning of winter that makes me automatically sad for some reason."

"What do you think it is?"

"I think it's a learned sadness," said Lucy. "I've actually had three serious relationships end around this time of year in my life. And my Dad died this time of year. It's just... I don't really have the Christmas spirit anymore. So a big snow storm like this, while I can appreciate its beauty, it also feels like a harbinger of things to come."

Aria was silent for a moment as she absorbed Lucy's words. Lucy looked over at her once again and smiled.

"I'm sorry," Lucy conferred. "I didn't mean to be such a downer. Let's not play that game. What are you going to do about your Dad?"

"I don't know," said Aria. "My Mom wants to put him in a nursing home. I just don't know if I'm ready for that."

"Yeah, but is he ready for that?" asked Lucy. "Maybe it is time, you know? Or maybe you could get a nurse to come by every day and help out."

"Maybe."

"If you don't want to talk about it, that's okay," Lucy consoled. "We can just drink our coffee and watch the storm together. I'm fine with that."

"I'm still figuring my feelings out," Aria said after a moment. "It's hard."

"I know."

They were both quiet once again. Lucy took a sip of coffee and bounced her eyes back and forth from Aria to the scene outside. There was a quiet, subtle pop song playing on the overhead speakers. Aria's eyes simply focused on the snow. She was lost in her own head.

Between five and six, the girls didn't have a single customer. Main Street had emptied of cars, apart from the occasional straggler who hadn't gotten home yet. At one point, a plow truck came barreling down Main, pushing the snow from the road aside and filling the street parking with it. The storm was not letting up. It was actually turning from a beautiful scene to something more concerning.

"I'm going to call Wendy," Aria said, lifting her phone up from the table. "I don't know if we should stay much longer."

"Good idea," said Lucy. "I hope we're able to get home."

"You can walk," replied Aria. Lucy smiled.

"Oh, right," she said. "Well, I worry about you."

Aria stuck her tongue out as she cradled her phone against her ear. She listened as it rang, and Lucy simply watched and sipped on her coffee.

"Hey," said Aria into the phone. "Yeah, just calling to check in."

"How's it looking there?" Wendy asked.

"It's dead," said Aria. "We haven't had a customer for an hour. And it's starting to look really bad out there."

"All right, close up," said Wendy. "If it starts to look dangerous out there, don't worry about not finishing the closing tasks. Just get the money in the safe and you get home safely."

"Cool, thanks Wendy," Aria replied. "I'll talk to you soon."

"Have a good night, Aria."

Aria hung up the phone and slipped it down onto the table. Lucy looked to Aria with a raised eyebrow.

"So we're good?" Lucy questioned.

"Yeah," said Aria, now standing up. "Let's get to closing this place down."

ONCE THE CAFE was cleaned up and shut down, the girls kicked through the snow on Main and made their way to Aria's car. Aria had offered Lucy a ride home, and while Lucy could certainly walk herself home, she was much more keen to spend a little more time with Aria. There were only a few cars out, driving through the snow and slush, a rare sight this early in the evening. But the snow was ceaseless, and it wasn't a great time to be out driving.

Aria's sedan was completely covered in snow where it was parked in the lot behind Main Street. There were a few other cars still parked there, all of them similarly covered. When the girls walked up to the car, all Aria could do was laugh.

"This is absurd," she said. "Do you see this?"

"Yep," Lucy replied with a laugh. She stepped up to Aria's car and used her forearm to knock the snow from one of the backseat windows. The thick, wet snow tumbled to the ground, as did a bit of snow from the roof.

"With the snow from last night," Aria said, kicking at some of the snow near her tire. "What is this? Like a foot?"

"I don't know," offered Lucy. "It's close."

"I don't know if my car is even capable of getting through this," Aria lamented. Her dark glasses were flecked with snowflakes. She had a look of disappointment on her face, a look of defeat. Lucy noticed it immediately and felt bad for her.

"Why don't we just walk to my place?" Lucy proposed. "Leave your car here. Fuck it. Even if we got it out, you know the roads are going to be garbage."

"But I need to get home to take care of my Dad," argued Aria. She was obviously torn from the expression on her face.

"Your Mom planned on you working until close tonight," Lucy pointed out. "She expected she'd have to make dinner and take care of him, right?"

"Right..."

"So it's okay," Lucy said with a smile and shrug. "Besides, your Mom is not going anywhere in this. And we shouldn't either. It'll probably be cleaned up by morning. We can dig your car out then."

Aria paused for a minute, considering Lucy's words. She stared at her car as she weighed the options. In the short time they had been standing there, a thin veil of snow had already peppered the backseat window that Lucy had brushed off.

"Okay," Aria said with acceptance after another moment of thought. "Okay, yeah. Let's just walk to your place."

Lucy smiled and nodded in agreement.

CHAPTER 10

*I*n the morning, Aria was the first to open her eyes. She was nuzzled up close to Lucy in bed, her hand lightly holding to Lucy's bare hip. A satisfied smile moved over Aria's face as she recognized where she was. Her eyes looked up and she saw the popcorn ceiling. A bright light shone between the slightly open blinds.

Trying not to disturb her lover, Aria peeled out from underneath the blanket, revealing her naked body. She shimmied out of bed and searched around for her clothes. First she found her underwear, laying near the foot of the bed, and she threaded herself into them. Next she slipped into her t-shirt. And finally, looking in Lucy's closet, she found a pair of sweatpants and put them on. Aria wiped at her eyes, missing her glasses. But her need to use the bathroom superseded her desire to see a little better.

The house felt cold as she tiptoed through the hallway. Although Lucy's Mom hadn't come home the previous night, Aria operated as though she could pop out at any moment. Lucy's house was much smaller than Aria's, and she knew she had to keep quiet if she didn't want to be discovered. Not that it mattered too much. Jean was a smart woman and she probably knew what was up. Still, Aria felt the need to sneak around, as if what she was doing—and the fact that she was there in the morning—was a big secret.

The only sound Aria made on her little morning adventure was the flushing of the toilet. And it was a loud flush. Despite this, she again tiptoed through the hallway, slinking around like a cat, and stepped her way back along the carpet to Lucy's room. As she neared the bedroom door, Aria got caught by the scene at the window. Outside was bright white, snow covering everything. The storm had ended, but in its wake was a deep, thick blanket of winter wonderland.

As Aria entered the room, the door creaked and she cringed slightly. Inside, Lucy was stirring in bed and she pushed herself up from the mattress. Aria smiled as she watched. Lucy adjusted the pillow behind herself so that she could sit up. The blanket fell from her chest, revealing her breasts and Aria smiled bigger. Then Lucy gave Aria a devilish look, she covered herself with the blanket once more, and patted the bed next to her. Aria dutifully trotted over.

"Can I have my glasses?" Aria asked.

"These?" teased Lucy, reaching over to the bedside table and plucking up Aria's black frames. She unfolded her arms and put them on her own face. Aria grinned.

"You look good," offered Aria.

"I think they look better on you," said Lucy, removing the glasses just as Aria hopped onto the bed at the foot and crawled up to her.

As Lucy handed the glasses over to Aria, the girls kissed delicately. Then Aria flipped over, sat up in bed next to Lucy, and put her glasses on.

"Did I wake you up?" asked Aria. "Your toilet is so loud." Lucy chuckled softly.

"No," said Lucy. "I was just waking up, too."

"I wasn't sure if your Mom was home or what," Aria went on. "I didn't want to wake her or run into her or anything."

"Oh, I forgot to tell you last night," said Lucy. "My Mom texted. She decided to stay at Paul's because of the storm."

"Ooh la la," Aria quipped in a sing-songy tone. Lucy laughed again.

"Scandalous," Lucy replied.

"I guess that means we're scandalous, too," Aria lobbed back.

"It certainly does."

"Hey, can you hand me my phone, too?" said Aria. "I haven't checked it since like seven last night."

"Sure," Lucy agreed. She took Aria's phone from the bedside table and handed it over. Aria took it with a smile, she pushed her glasses up her nose, and she looked down into the screen.

Lucy watched as Aria's expression went from happy to perplexed.

"Is something wrong?" Lucy asked.

"I don't know," Aria said solemnly. She tapped on her phone screen a couple of times. "My Mom tried to call me a few times last night. She texted, too."

"What did she say?"

"'Can you call me asap?,'" Aria read.

"Oh," said Lucy. "Okay, well, maybe you should call her now."

"Right," said Aria.

She had a pained and worried look on her face as she tapped on her phone and then brought it up to her ear. Lucy crossed her arms and watched in silence.

"Mom," said Aria into her phone. "What's going on?"

Aria listened and Lucy watched. Aria's eyebrows shifted and her eyes grew bigger.

"Wait, what?" Aria questioned with greater urgency. "Are you serious? Oh my God."

Aria looked to Lucy, and she looked as though she were about to cry. Lucy could feel her heart racing. She knew exactly what was going on, and in a preemptive move, she reached over and took Aria's hand. Lucy squeezed.

"Mom, I just..." said Aria. "I... can't... I... I'm sorry. I'm so sorry."

Lucy felt a tear coming to her own eye and she quickly wiped at it. But a few more begin to well up in her eyes as she saw tears rolling down Aria's cheeks.

"Okay," said Aria. "My car is still on Main Street. I have to dig it out. I stayed over at Lucy's last night after work because the storm had gotten so bad. But I'll be home as soon as I can. Okay? I'm sorry. This is just... this is fucked."

Lucy squeezed Aria's hand once more.

"Yeah," Aria continued. "Okay. Yes, I love you, too. I'll see you soon."

Aria pulled the phone from her ear and looked down into the screen as she pushed the button to end the call. She sighed as a few more tears left her eyes and rained down to her chin. Then she looked over to Lucy.

"My Dad died last night," Aria said with finality. She dropped her phone to the bed and collapsed into Lucy. Lucy wrapped an arm around her and held her, whispering condolences into Aria's ear softly as she cried.

ALL BUNDLED up in their winter wear, Lucy and Aria trudged through the deep snow and slowly made their way toward the parking lot behind Main Street. On any regular day, there would be cars driving and people milling about. But it was as if Madeira was shut down. The plows were out, doing their best to clear the roads, along with the occasional pickup truck that could navigate through the mess. When the girls reached Main, they crossed the street despite the green light. No cars where coming from either direction.

"I knew it was coming," Aria offered through her sadness. "It's not a surprise. He hadn't been doing well. But it hurts."

"I know," consoled Lucy, huddled up in her winter coat next to Aria. "I'm so sorry."

"I should have been there," said Aria. "I feel so irresponsible. I'm off having a great night with my girlfriend, only thinking about myself, when I really should have been there."

Despite the sad circumstances, Lucy smiled gently at Aria calling her her girlfriend. Lucy threaded her arm into Aria's, and the girls continued their walk with arms linked.

"It actually makes me angry," Aria went on. "Because I know how my Mom has been through all this, and I can't help but feel she ignored something or neglected him in some way."

"No," countered Lucy. "You can't think about it like that, Aria. That's unfair."

Aria was silent for a few moments.

"I know," she said after she reflected on her own words. "I'm just hurt. I'm just really fucking sad."

"There's your car," Lucy replied, pointing out to a mound of snow with a few car-looking parts sticking out. She looked to Aria and smiled.

Aria slowly smiled back.

"My fucking car," mused Aria.

Together, the girls tackled the car with zeal. Aria let Lucy use the sole snow brush, while she herself used her hands and arms to clear snow off of her car. The sky was clear and blue, with a bright sun overhead, but it was still quite frigid in temperature. At one point during the exercise in snow removal, Aria found herself lost in the act, smiling as she and Lucy dug the car out.

Aria brushed the caked snow off of her arms and then rubbed her gloved hands together. She opened the driver side door and sat down on the seat. After kicking her boots off, she slid her legs inside and looked around the car. The windows were clear and the sun was shining in. In the rear view mirror, she could see Lucy still brushing snow off from the trunk.

"Here we go," Aria said. She plugged her key into the ignition and turned it. The car roared to life.

Outside, Lucy looked on at her job and decided it to be finished. Walking around the car, she moved to the passenger side, she opened the door, and she got in. Lucy tossed the snow brush to the floor in the backseat and then she smiled at Aria.

"Think you can get out?" Lucy asked.

"Well, we dug around the tires as best as we could," replied Aria. "I guess we'll see."

Aria put the car into reverse, put her hand behind Lucy's seat and turned her head. She gave the car some gas and, sure enough, it crunched over the snow. Both Lucy and Aria cheered happily. Then Aria shifted gears into drive and stepped on the gas, only to find her wheels spinning.

"Damn," Aria huffed.

"Don't worry," Lucy said with a smile, unfastening her seat belt. "I'll push."

With Lucy behind the car pushing and Aria driving, they

moved through the unplowed parking lot slowly and carefully. But it wasn't long before they reached the street, which had been plowed. Lucy bounced around the car once more and hopped into the passenger side. Once she was back in with her seat belt fastened, Aria smiled to her and lifted a palm up. Lucy high-fived her in celebration, and then Aria resumed driving, turning onto the street and rolling down the slushy pavement, on her way home to deal with the inevitability of life.

The girls were silent for a while, as Aria concentrated on driving and Lucy looked out the window at all the snow. It was one of the snowfalls that made everything feel so quiet, like the world was shut down. It was comforting. Lucy had so much on her mind lately, that all this—the storm, Aria's Dad's passing, the task of digging the car out—took her out of her thoughts and let her concentrate on the present. It was selfish, sure, but it made her feel sane, in a way. It made her feel grounded.

"Hey," said Lucy suddenly, breaking the silence.

"Yeah?" replied Aria with a gentle inquisitiveness in her voice.

"When you called me your girlfriend earlier, on our walk downtown," Lucy admitted. "It made me feel really good."

A soft smile came over Aria's face.

"It's been a little while since I had a girlfriend," Lucy went on. "And with everything that's been going in in my life, with all the changes I've had to endure... it's just... it's nice. It makes me really happy."

"It makes me happy, too," said Aria. "To have you. Especially right now." Reaching her hand over, Aria searched for

Lucy's hand. Lucy took her hand in turn, and she squeezed it. A single tear came to Aria's eye.

"It's going to be okay," said Lucy. "I'm here for you. I know how you're feeling, I've been there. And I'm here for you."

"Thank you," Aria replied in a low tone. "It really means a lot to me. Thank you, Lucy."

Lucy smiled and nodded. She squeezed Aria's hand again before they released one another. Aria's hand went back to the wheel, and Lucy's went up to her own cheek. She rubbed her face delicately, and her eyes resumed watching the white landscape pass by outside.

———

Lucy followed behind Aria as they entered Aria's house. They were both solemn and silent, and although she wanted to support her girlfriend, Lucy felt out of place and anxious for being there. It felt like a family matter, like something more personal, and that she really shouldn't be in attendance. It also felt weird that while she had met Aria's mother before, never had she met her with Aria present. And that previous meeting had obviously been under some more surreptitious circumstances.

"Wait," Lucy said suddenly. Aria stopped.

"Yeah?"

"I feel a little weird about this," Lucy admitted. "I mean, I'm here for you. I want to be here for you. But I don't know if I belong in the conversation with you."

"Right," Aria said. "That makes sense."

"I'm sorry," offered Lucy. "Really."

"Why don't you just head up to my bedroom," replied Aria. "I'll talk to my Mom and then I'll come up. Does that work?"

"Yeah, sure," said Lucy, nodding in agreement. "I'll do that."

"Okay," said Aria. She smiled gently and then she leaned in and kissed Lucy. "I'll see you in a few."

The girls broke from one another, Lucy heading up the staircase and Aria continuing down the hallway toward the kitchen. As Lucy approached the landing upstairs, she noticed that she could see over the open railing down into the living room and into the kitchen. There stood Aria's mother Phyllis, looking through some paperwork and standing at the kitchen counter. While Lucy knew she should continue on to Aria's room, she couldn't help herself. She sat down on the carpet and put her face against the railing. She waited and watched as Aria arrived in the kitchen.

"Mom," said Aria as she entered.

"Aria," replied Phyllis. She sighed. "I'm so sorry."

"What happened?" Aria went on, stepping closer to her mother. She crossed her arms and tried to hold it together.

"The doctor said he had had a few mini strokes earlier on in the day," said Phyllis with a look of seriousness in her eyes. "And then a much larger one later on. That's when I noticed and called the ambulance. They had difficulty getting here in the snow last night. He died soon after arriving at the hospital."

"Oh my God," said Aria. She put her hand on her head as she absorbed the news. "I should have been here."

"There's nothing you could have done, sweetie," said Phyllis. "It was just his time. We knew that he was getting worse."

"I know," Aria agreed. "But I should have been here."

"Come here, Aria," Phyllis said, opening her arms. Aria moved closer to her and, for the first time in a while, hugged her mother.

"I just should have been here."

Lucy watched from above, wiping a tear from her eye. It was a difficult scene to absorb. She had missed the death of her own father, and it had plagued Lucy for some time. In a way, she knew just what Aria was going through. Lucy always regretted not being there more for her mother when her father died. She was absorbed in her life in New York. She should have been there.

"So what's next?" Aria asked after a moment, stepping back from their embrace. She rubbed her finger across her cheek to remove a tear.

"He's going to be cremated," Phyllis affirmed. "We'll hold a service at the funeral home in town."

"Okay," said Aria with a slow nod.

"We'll have some paperwork to go through," continued Phyllis. "That's what I'm looking through here. Some legal issues to address. His will is pretty straightforward and clear, but there's always something. I'll be speaking with our attorney a little bit later today."

"Okay," said Aria again.

"I'll need your assistance in going through his things," Phyllis proposed. "His workshop in the basement. His memorabilia. We should have addressed that some time ago, of course, but I admit it felt strange considering downsizing his possessions when he was still with us."

"I can help go through it all," Aria agreed.

"Good," said Phyllis. "Maybe we'll hold a garage sale or something. Or sell some of the more valuable items online. You know, I do know a very good estate sale company, so maybe we'll go that route."

"I want to look through it all," said Aria firmly.

"Yes," said Phyllis. "Well, after that, maybe an estate sale is the way to go. Regardless, I think you should start getting it in your mind to look for a house of your own. Now that Theo has passed, I plan to sell this house and downsize to a condo."

"Already?" asked Aria. "So fast?"

"This house is far too big for me, Aria," said Phyllis. "And you are an adult woman. You shouldn't be living at home with your mother any longer."

Aria suddenly felt shameful, and upstairs Lucy had some feelings about this statement as well.

"Besides, you will have the money to do so," Phyllis went on. "Obviously I will help you. Madeira is a hot location, houses sell fast, and it would certainly be a good investment for you. A smaller, starter home would be a great buy."

"Okay, Mom," Aria said through a sigh.

"Just please... start thinking about it," Phyllis said with

finality. "I'm going to get back to this paperwork. Maybe you and I could go out for dinner later."

"I don't know if I'll be hungry."

"Well, just let me know, sweetie," Phyllis conferred.

"Thanks," said Aria. She huffed in resignation and turned from her mother, walking back down the hallway and toward the stairs. As she did this, Lucy popped up from where she sat on the carpet and stepped closer to the top of the stairs, waiting for Aria to ascend.

When Aria saw Lucy waiting for her above, she smiled softly. Though it was obvious that she had been tearing up.

The girls sat together in Aria's room, Lucy on the small sofa, and Aria perched crosslegged on the floor across from her. Aria looked defeated. There was sadness in her face, but her expression conveyed more demoralization than anything. Lucy felt for her, and tried to remain positive.

"I can help you go through his things," offered Lucy. "We could do it together."

"Thank you," said Aria solemnly.

"And really, anything else you need," continued Lucy. "Just tell me. And I'll do it."

Aria looked up to her and smiled.

"Thank you," she said again.

"I don't know when the appropriate time to tell you this is," said Lucy. "Or was. But I sort of went out of my way to meet your Mom a little while ago."

"You did?" asked Aria, her interest piqued.

"Yeah, I did," admitted Lucy. "I was out for a run some time back, I saw an open house with a sign out front that had your Mom's picture on it. So I went in and pretended I was house shopping."

Aria smiled once more.

"It was stupid," said Lucy. "I just wanted to meet her and see for myself if she was like you said. And she was. I'm sorry I didn't tell you. I felt kind of bad about it after the fact. A little embarrassed, like I was snooping around."

"It's okay," Aria comforted. "I don't really care. But now when you meet her with me, you're going to have some explaining to do."

"That's why I brought it up," Lucy went on. "I figure, I'm going to be meeting her with you very soon."

"Yeah, and my Mom doesn't really know that I'm gay, if you remember," Aria added. "Bit of a pickle we're in, I think."

"Yeah," Lucy agreed.

"Well, fuck it for now," said Aria. "We'll slip out of here today. But I mean... you're going to come with me to the funeral, right?"

"Yes, of course I will," said Lucy without hesitation. "I will definitely be there."

"So you'll have to meet her then," Aria posited. "I mean, you didn't pretend to be someone you're not, did you? Apart from looking for a house..."

"No, I told her my name was Lucille," said Lucy.

"Which is true."

"Right," Lucy agreed.

"You know, she might not even remember you," Aria proposed. "I think we'll be fine."

"What about coming out to her?"

"Not at his funeral," Aria said, now standing up from the floor. "It's not the place."

"Okay," said Lucy.

Aria crossed her arms and sighed. Then something hit her. She quickly reached into her pocket and retrieved her phone.

"Damn it, I have to work in like an hour," she said with disappointment. "Just... fuck!"

"Maybe it'll be good for you," said Lucy. "Maybe it'll take your mind off it all."

"Maybe."

Aria walked to the large window in the middle of her room and looked outside. Across the street, two kids were rolling large snowballs. They were making a snowman, and it was the perfect day for that kind of thing. She wished everything were simpler. Simpler times. She didn't want to go into work. She didn't want to think about her father's death. She just wanted to make a snowman with Lucy.

But life wasn't always so simple.

CHAPTER 11

*L*ucy fed the last few dirty dishes into the dishwasher and closed the door. She pushed in a button and turned a knob, and the dishwasher came to life with a whirring sound. It wasn't the greatest appliance, a cheap dishwasher that her Mom had installed over a decade ago, but it did the trick. After wiping her hands on a towel and hanging that towel on the oven handle, Lucy meandered out of the kitchen and into her living room.

By chance, she noticed that her phone was ringing on the coffee table. It was on silent, but she could see the screen light up. Lucy walked over to the table and picked up her phone, looking down into the screen. She raised her brow in confusion. It was an old coworker of hers, Lorna, from New York. They had both been laid off at the same time. It felt out of place for Lorna to be calling her.

"Hello?" Lucy said cautiously as she answered.

"Merry Christmas!" bleated Lorna on the other end. "Well, Merry almost-Christmas." Lucy chuckled softly.

"Yeah, Merry Christmas to you, too," Lucy replied. "How are you, Lorna?"

"I'm good, Lucy," offered Lorna. "I'm really good. It's been a strange year, but I'm doing great now."

"Hey, that's good to hear," said Lucy.

"I bet you're wondering why I'm calling."

"You are correct," Lucy confirmed.

"It's out of the blue, I know," Lorna admitted. "But here's the deal. A few months back I landed a job in account management at another marketing agency in the City. Gawain International. Heard of it?"

"It sounds familiar," mused Lucy.

"We handle advertising and marketing for primarily fast food brands," Lorna continued. "The big ones. Burger Baron. Taco Hut."

"Wow, okay," said Lucy. "That's great, Lorna. Congratulations."

"Well, I'm not calling to brag or anything," Lorna continued with a laugh. "I'm calling because I remembered how fucking ridiculous it was that good, hardworking people like you and I got laid off. So when my boss asked me if I knew anyone who was looking for a job, I immediately thought of you."

"Lorna, I'm shook," Lucy said in earnest. "That's so sweet of you. It's amazing."

"I'm just an amazing gal, I know," Lorna quipped with another laugh. "So if you can get me your resume right away, I'll forward it on to my boss and I'm sure they'll be in touch fast. They recently cleared house and have some positions to fill."

"That's... that's great," Lucy replied with trepidation. "The only problem is that I don't live in New York anymore. I left."

"You left?" Lorna barked back skeptically. "Where did you go?"

"I went back home," said Lucy. "To Michigan."

"I mean, is that where you want to stay?" asked Lorna. "In Michigan?"

"I don't know."

"Okay, look," Lorna surmised. "Send me your resume, like, now. As soon as we get off the phone. And when they call you, get a damn plane ticket and come out here and interview. The Lucy I know loves New York City. You're a city girl, through and through. This is your home. Come back to your real home."

Lucy paused and considered what Lorna was proposing.

"I'm about to run into a meeting," Lorna went on with urgency. "Send me your resume. Do it. I promise you'll get a call. A month from now, you could be the account manager for one of the biggest chains in the country. This is a huge opportunity."

"Okay," said Lucy. "I'll send it after we get off the phone."

"You have my email address?"

"Yes, I'm sure I do."

"Wonderful," beamed Lorna. "Thanks Lucy. I can't wait

to work with you again. And if I don't talk to you again before the holidays, Merry Christmas!"

"Yeah," said Lucy. "Merry Christmas."

Lorna disconnected. Removing the phone from her ear, Lucy looked down into the screen. She knew she should be jumping for joy, but instead she just felt like shit.

LUCY SAT by herself a few rows from the front, wearing a black dress, black leggings, and black boots. She held a program in her hands and went back and forth from skimming through it to looking around the funeral home at the various guests in attendance. Up at the front of the room there was a table, and on that table there was both an urn and a folded American flag in a wooden box. Next to the table there was a lectern with a microphone jutting up from it.

She felt out of place. She felt lonely and exposed. Lucy only wished for Aria to join her. But Aria was sauntering around the funeral home, speaking to friends and family, rising to the duty of being the daughter of the deceased. When Lucy did see Aria, she appeared brave and courageous. Lucy knew it was difficult for her. Aria loved her father dearly, and his death was a substantial blow to her. And all of this, inevitably, reminded Lucy of her own father's passing. In fact, the anniversary of her dad's death was just over a week away.

Looking down into the program again, Lucy began

reading Theodore Caspar's biography. But this was soon interrupted by a person moving into Lucy's periphery.

"Pardon me," said a familiar voice. Lucy looked up to find Aria's mother Phyllis hovering over her.

"Oh, hello," offered Lucy.

"We've met before," Phyllis said with a finger lifted. "Did you come to an open house of mine some time ago?"

Lucy folded the program and put it down into her lap. Then she softly smiled up at Phyllis.

"Yes, I do believe so," said Lucy.

"Remind me of your name again?"

"Lucy," she replied. "Lucille."

"Ah yes!" said Phyllis as it all became clear. "I do remember you. Did you... know my husband?"

"No," said Lucy. "Not really. I'm a friend of Aria's, actually. I, um... work with her at the coffee shop."

"I see," Phyllis said. She paused for a moment. "Are you still looking for a house?"

"I'm not sure," Lucy replied. "I'm sorry. I'm sorry for your loss."

"Yes, thank you."

"But when I am looking again," Lucy went on. "I'll be in touch with you."

"That's great to hear," Phyllis said with a small smile. "Thank you for coming."

"It's no problem."

Phyllis offered Lucy another smile before turning and moving away from her. Exhaling a sigh of relief, Lucy once again looked around for Aria, eager for her to join her.

Aria, meanwhile, was standing in the hallway talking to a man who had about twenty years on her. She wore black slacks, a black jacket, and had her blonde hair tied up in a bun. With a solemn look on her face, she spoke to the man, with whom she was quite familiar.

"It's been a rough year, Jacob," she admitted. "He had just been going downhill quickly. It happened so fast, I really couldn't believe it."

"I'm sorry we haven't been more helpful," Jacob offered. "But being out of state and all, I don't know how much we could have been of service."

"It's okay," said Aria.

"I really haven't been the best son these last few years," Jacob continued. "It's a source of shame for me, to be quite honest."

"No," Aria countered. "Please don't think like that. You couldn't uproot you and your family's lives for this. I appreciate you being here now."

"Thank you, Aria," replied Jacob. It was obvious from his expression that he still felt ashamed. "Have you talked to James and Linda yet?"

"Yes, I have," Aria said. "I explained to them how the will divides everything among us kids. Are you available for a quick meeting with the lawyer tomorrow morning?"

"I am," said Jacob. "Thank you for handling all this, Aria. We're all very lucky to have you in this family."

"Thanks Jacob."

"I'm going to go talk to your mother," Jacob said, putting his hand on Aria's arm. "I'll see you in there."

"All right," replied Aria. She smiled gently. Jacob nodded and returned her smile, then he ambled off.

Turning around, Aria went to scan the small crowd to see who else was in attendance that she should talk to. But looking through the doorway into the parlor room, she spotted Lucy looking in her direction. Aria smiled and offered a small wave to Lucy, and Lucy did the same in return. After a moment of hesitation, Aria picked up her feet and walked toward where Lucy sat.

"Hey," Aria said as she approached Lucy.

"Hey," replied Lucy. "You doing okay?"

"I'm okay," admitted Aria. "It's hard, you know, but I knew this was all coming."

"So I 'met' your mother," Lucy said. Aria smiled.

"Yeah? How did that go?"

"She wanted to know if I was still interested in buying a house," quipped Lucy. Aria let out a small laugh, but quickly stifled it.

"Cute," Aria retorted. "Well, whatever. At the very least, my Dad's death is about to shake some things up."

"But hey," Lucy said again, this time reaching out and taking Aria's hand. "Are you actually doing okay?"

"Yes," Aria reaffirmed. "Surprisingly. I feel a sense of closure, in a way. And kind of... liberated? Maybe that's not the right word."

"No, I think that's appropriate."

"I've put a lot of my life on hold," Aria went on. "And now it seems like... I can do whatever I like. It's like I've been released from my charge. It's an odd sense of freedom that I haven't felt in a very long time."

Lucy smiled and squeezed Aria's hand.

"What's the first thing you want to do with your newfound freedom?" asked Lucy.

"Kiss you in public," Aria intoned. Smiling, she leaned down and planted a gentle and adoring kiss on Lucy's lips. Lucy smiled brightly.

"How did that feel?" Lucy replied.

"Wonderful," said Aria. She looked around. "And nobody even noticed."

"As it should be," said Lucy. "There's nothing wrong with it."

"That's true," Aria agreed. Looking toward the door, Aria noticed a short, slim man entering whom she recognized. "I think we're about to start the service. That's one of the funeral home employees."

"Oh," Lucy said, looking in the same direction as Aria. "Okay, well, good luck... or, break a leg. I don't know what to say to someone about to give a speech at a funeral."

"Thank you," Aria said with a smile. She twirled a strand of Lucy's hair in her fingers. "I appreciate you being here for me."

Lucy nodded and returned her girlfriend's smile.

With that, Aria walked off from Lucy and up toward the front of the room where she met with the funeral home employee. They spoke to one another, and Lucy watched with interest. She felt for Aria, as Aria was a good person who had been tested so much. To see Aria endure through her trials with such resiliency was an inspiration to Lucy. It got the wheels in her brain turning.

The man from the funeral home then approached the microphone at the lectern and looked out into the crowd of people milling about.

"Attention please," he said in amplification. "Please take your seats, as the service is soon to begin."

Aria looked out to Lucy and smiled. Lucy smiled back. Despite the circumstances, they both felt happy in that moment.

LATER ON THAT NIGHT, Lucy stood alone in her house, cradling a glass of wine in her hand, staring out of the window. The snow was still piled up outside, though the roads and sidewalk had been cleared. It looked as quiet outside as it felt inside. Her Mom, falling deep into her new love affair, was spending another evening with her beau. And Lucy was envious, wanting nothing more than to be spending time with her new lover. Taking a sip of wine, Lucy wished Aria was there with her. But she knew Aria had so much more to attend to.

Lucy turned from the window and slunk across the carpet in her pajamas. She felt restless and lost. There was a lot on her mind to parse out, and she hadn't made any firm decisions yet. How could she? It felt as though there was no right answer. She had indeed forwarded her resume to Lorna, and though she hadn't heard anything back yet, she knew a call was inevitable. But now the thought of leaving Madeira and returning to New York wasn't as appetizing as it once was. Lucy didn't know how to feel. So she just took another sip of wine and crumbled down onto the couch.

It was then that some headlights shown in through the front window. Lucy perked up, wondering why her Mom had come home so soon after she texted saying she would probably be sleeping over at Paul's again. Lucy picked herself up from the couch once more, and returned to the front window.

And when she arrived at the window, she saw that familiar old tan luxury sedan and she watched as Aria climbed out of it, still dressed in her clothes from the funeral earlier. Lucy's eyes widened, and her smile grew bigger still as Aria walked up the pathway to the front door.

With a revitalized eagerness, Lucy yanked the front door open and grinned wildly as Aria approached. Aria saw Lucy waiting for her, and she smiled as well. Stepping closer, Aria kissed Lucy, and then they hugged tightly.

"I'm so happy you came over," intoned Lucy longingly through their embrace.

"I saw your text," said Aria. "Sorry I didn't respond. It was a busy day."

"I can imagine," Lucy replied. She stepped back from their hug, still maintaining a smile. "Come on in."

Aria, still smiling as well, did as was requested.

"Can I get you a glass of wine?" asked Lucy, picking up her own glass and taking a sip.

"No," said Aria. "It's been fun experimenting with

drinking again, but I think it'll take me down a road I have no interest in traveling. If that makes sense."

"It does," Lucy confirmed.

Aria removed her coat, hung it on the coat rack, and then also removed her black jacket and hung that as well. She kicked off her pumps and then moved into the living room, dressed in socks, slacks, and a button-down blouse. Lucy was finding her comfort on the couch, and Aria followed her lead, sitting on a folded leg next to Lucy.

"So?" asked Lucy. "How was the rest of the day?"

"Exhausting," Aria said. "And my brain just won't stop processing. I've got even more to do tomorrow. We've got a meeting with the lawyer about the will."

"In this kind of situation," Lucy began. "Wouldn't everything just go to your mother for now?"

"Well, no," replied Aria. "It's a bit more complicated than that because of my Dad's other kids. So how it's constructed, basically, is that my Mom is getting 50% of his estate, and the other 50% is split between me and my three step-siblings."

"Ah," said Lucy in understanding.

"The house is also completely owned by my Mom," Aria went on. "But she's planning to sell that anyway, as you know."

"Right."

"Even so," said Aria. "My inheritance will be considerable. And legally I'll finally be able to take full ownership of my trust fund. It's just a lot to wrap my brain around. Especially because I really don't care about the money."

"But at the same time," proposed Lucy. "You could do a lot of good for yourself with it."

"That's true," agreed Aria. "But I can't help but feel like... like kind of an orphan right now. I don't have the greatest relationship with my mother, and I know she's going to be off doing her own thing from here on out. I'm also not super close with my step-siblings. Jacob lives out of state. James and Linda both live out in Grand Rapids. They're not really part of my life. With my Dad now gone... I just..."

Aria lowered her head and immediately Lucy put an arm around her to console her.

"It's all right," cooed Lucy sympathetically. "It's really hard to lose a parent."

"It's a lot to absorb, you know?" intoned Aria, wiping at her eye underneath her glasses.

Lucy kissed Aria's head and held her for a few moments, letting Aria just be and have the feelings she needed to feel. But soon enough, Aria lifted her head with a reinvigorated sense of duty.

"I know that my Dad wouldn't want me to crumble under the weight of all this," Aria continued. "He was the kind of man who faced things head-on and that's how he taught me to be. To be positive and optimistic in the face of adversity. Part of being a good person is to not let yourself spiral downward when you're in a hole. You've got to look up to get out of that hole."

"When I saw you today at the funeral," Lucy began. "You were inspirational. You were brave when others might collapse. I knew what you were going through—I've been there—and yet you were able to hold your head high and do what was required of you. And your eulogy was equally inspirational. I can tell that you are your father's daughter."

"Thank you," Aria replied, leaning into Lucy. They held one another's hand, fingers threaded together. Aria was grateful to be in the calm of her lover's presence after such a tense and tiring day. What they had together was really flourishing, that was obvious to the both of them.

"I don't mean to spoil this moment," Lucy injected carefully. "But there's just something on my mind that I need to tell you."

"Okay," Aria replied softly. She sat upright and looked at Lucy with a weary smile.

"Yesterday I got a call from a friend in New York," said Lucy. "I used to work with her. Anyway, she was essentially calling me with a job opportunity doing something similar to what I used to do at my old company. She asked me to send her my resume. And I did."

"Oh," Aria intoned. She looked away for a moment as the thought sunk in. "So... I mean... what's going to happen?"

"I don't know," replied Lucy. "I've been just so worried for so long, you know? It's been impossible for me to find a job for so long. Now things seem to be turning a corner, and this opportunity falls in my lap. Back in New York, no less. But..." she said and paused, trying to find the appropriate words. "I'm starting to finally feel like I'm a part of Madeira somehow. I'm reconnecting with my Mom. And now I've got you."

Aria smiled and nodded.

"I'm just so torn," Lucy went on. "I miss New York. I miss my old life there. But I can't help but feel that it's just the past, and the future holds something different for me."

"The past is already gone, the future is not yet here," offered Aria. "There's only one moment for you to live, and that is the present moment."

"Did you just come up with that?" asked Lucy. Aria laughed softly.

"No, the Buddha said that," she replied.

"Oh," Lucy said with a sheepish smile.

"Well, if you ask me," continued Aria. "I think you should stay right here." She snuggled once more into Lucy with loving affection, and Lucy returned the gesture.

"This has been a hard year," Lucy said.

"Yeah, it has," Aria agreed. "But right now is okay."

"Right now is okay," said Lucy. She laid her head on Aria's shoulder. The cold outside couldn't permeate the warmth between them. This was the house in which Lucy grew up, and no matter what she did, it would always be home.

CHAPTER 12

There was a lull in customers at Fair Grounds, and Lucy stood at the counter with a dazed, blank face. Her mind was wandering, trying to put together the pieces of her life, trying to calculate what she wanted. There was so much to consider. And while only a couple months ago she might have known exactly how to proceed, now it wasn't so clear cut. Everything felt murky.

"Do you have your tree up yet?" asked a voice in Lucy's periphery.

"Huh?" mused Lucy, breaking from her reverie and turning. Standing next to her was a smiling Wendy.

"Your tree?" repeated Wendy. "Did you and your Mom put up your Christmas tree yet?"

"Oh," replied Lucy, back in reality. "You know, my Mom stopped putting a tree up years ago after my Dad passed. I was in New York and didn't come home for Christmas. So it just didn't really make sense anymore, I guess."

"That's too bad," said Wendy. "But since you're living at home now, maybe now's a good time to bring the tradition back?"

"I don't know," said Lucy. "Maybe."

"One of my favorite parts of Christmas is putting up my tree with my kids," Wendy continued. "It just makes me feel... love." She smiled.

Lucy paused and smiled gently, too.

"That's a nice sentiment," Lucy conferred. "But I just don't know if we can go back to that. It's a different time."

"Yeah, I know," said Wendy. She smiled again and shrugged.

Just then, Lucy felt her phone vibrate in her pocket. Slipping it out of her jeans, Lucy looked down into the screen and tapped. There was a text message from Lorna.

"Check your email," Lorna had texted.

"Hey, excuse me for a second," Lucy said to Wendy.

"Okay, no problem," Wendy replied with a smile. She turned from Lucy and walked over to the espresso machine, where she began giving it a wipe down.

Lucy tapped a few more times into her phone and navigated to her email. When her new messages loaded up, there was one titled, 'Scheduling an interview' from a woman named Jenny Reed. Lucy opened the message and carefully read the contents. Her eyes widened. It was indeed an offer to schedule an interview with Lorna's company. It was the first real interview she had been offered since the economy had faltered and she lost her job. It felt like coming up for air after a long, long time under water.

Looking up, Lucy searched around the coffee shop. It was quiet but for the low beat of the music coming through the speakers overhead. There were a few customers at tables, all absorbed in their own things. And there was Wendy, standing at the espresso machine, rubbing a white towel up and down the milk steamer nozzle. Lucy wanted to celebrate. She wanted to scream out loud. But it felt inappropriate. It felt unimportant. It felt inconsequential.

Lucy sighed and put her phone away. She looked over to Wendy once more and Wendy caught her gaze. Wendy smiled, and Lucy smiled in kind.

When her shift came to an end, Lucy bid farewell to Wendy, wrapped herself up in her winter gear, and stepped out onto Main Street into the cold. She suddenly realized that Main was bustling with the pre-Christmas crowd. Groups were happily strolling by, carrying packages, bundled up in puffy coats and scarves. The holiday had completely snuck up on her. It was as though it came out of nowhere. It had been such a strange year.

As she walked toward the crosswalk, weaving in and out of gaggles of people, Lucy recounted what her life was like last Christmas. She remembered the party at her office, filled with drunken revelry. They were drinking gin martinis and she ended up stumbling down the street with a few of her coworkers, smoking cigarettes and screeching into the night. But on Christmas day, she was alone in her Brooklyn apartment, counting the minutes until noon so that she could pour herself a drink and not feel shame about it. She would call her Mom, talk for about fifteen minutes, and then spend the rest of the day watching movies by herself.

Being back in Madeira, she had healed herself. Somewhat, at least. She certainly wasn't drinking like she had been back in New York. Her diet was a bit better. And she was running for a while, before all the snow arrived. Lucy had actually lost a few inches around her middle. Maybe it was the lack of stress from her old job that helped. Maybe it was the cleaner lifestyle. Or maybe it was because she was starting to feel happier.

As the light changed and the walk sign appeared, Lucy sauntered across the street with her hands pushed into her pockets, head down and watching her feet move in front of her. Then, suddenly, she thought she heard something behind her. It almost sounded like her name.

"Lucy! Hey Lucy, wait up!"

Turning her head to look behind her, Lucy saw Aria speeding through the crosswalk. Lucy's face brightened up and she smiled wide. When Aria reached her, she wrapped both arms around Lucy and gripped tightly, and Lucy returned the gesture with a hug of her own. The girls laughed together.

"Hey!" said Lucy with a newfound excitement. "What are you doing?"

"Let's keep walking," Aria countered. "That light is going to change in no time."

"Right," Lucy replied with another laugh. Together, the girls rushed out of the road and made it to the other side before their turn to walk expired.

"I was coming to meet you at the end of your shift," said Aria, adjusting her glasses slightly. "But I was running a bit late."

"Did the meeting with the lawyer go long?" asked Lucy.

"Oh, not particularly," replied Aria. "But we all went out for lunch afterwards. That went a little longer than I expected. It was nice to really catch up with my step-siblings. I hadn't been together with all of them like that in a long time."

"That's nice," Lucy said and smiled. "So everything went as expected otherwise?"

"It did," confirmed Aria. She smiled back and shrugged.

"Well... great!" beamed Lucy. "I'm glad things are sorting themselves out."

"Thanks," said Aria. "It's really just nice to have that taken care of so I can start to move past this dark, dark time. I still feel so gutted, you know? But now I feel like I can really start to heal."

"That's a great attitude and a great way to look at it," said Lucy. She looked around where they stood and thought to herself for a moment. "You know, I was heading home but we can stay downtown for a little while if you want."

"No, let's go to your house," said Aria happily. "I'll walk with you."

"But isn't your car down here?"

Aria waved off Lucy's concerns. Then she threaded her arm into Lucy's and tugged, continuing Lucy's path away from Main Street, and off toward her house on Elm.

Their conversation was lively and upbeat on the way to

Lucy's house, with laughter peppered in and positivity throughout. Lucy told Aria about her job interview, and Aria congratulated her, urging her to at least do the interview and see what happened. But Lucy felt conflicted about it, especially as she walked arm-in-arm with the woman who she knew she was completely falling for. Aria's insistence was genuine, but it still didn't make Lucy feel much better about her ensuing decisions.

When they arrived at home, Jean's car was parked in the driveway and the girls smiled at one another. They walked together up to the front door, and as Lucy searched her coat for the house keys, Aria popped in and stole a kiss from her. Lucy laughed and the girls kissed a few more times before Lucy finally inserted the key into the door, unlocked it, and turned the knob.

Inside the house was warm and inviting. Lucy and Aria began to remove their coats and kick off their boots, talking the entire time. This commotion stirred Jean from the other room. And she approached them in the hallway with a curious smile on her face.

"Well, good afternoon, ladies," Jean offered with a hint of irony. "You both seam in good spirits."

"We're all right," replied Lucy. "Considering the circumstances."

Jean lifted an eyebrow and looked between the two.

"My, um... my Dad passed away a few days ago," Aria said with a hint of sheepishness. She felt guilty about acting so jovial with her father's death so recent.

"My God," Jean gasped. "Dear, I am so sorry for your

loss." Jean rushed forward and she grabbed Aria, hugging her tightly.

"Thank you," Aria squeaked out, returning Jean's hug.

"You're very brave," Jean went on. "To continue living your best life in the face of such difficulty. I've been there. When we lost Lucy's father, I was heartbroken. But perseverance is the only way."

"Thank you," repeated Aria, patting Jean on the back. Jean released her and smiled a pained smile.

"Aria has been very brave," Lucy conferred. "She's a strong woman."

"Surely," agreed Jean.

"You're both very sweet," said Aria. "But I don't deserve any special praise. Truly, I've only done what was my duty."

Jean looked to Lucy and smiled a knowing smile.

"So as not to embarrass Aria anymore than she probably already feels," Lucy pivoted. "Mom, I feel like I haven't seen you in some time."

"I—" countered Jean quickly, and then she paused to consider her words. "Yes, I've been coming and going a lot recently."

Lucy raised an eyebrow. She looked a lot like her mother with this expression on her face.

"Things with Paul have been going quite well," Jean said matter-of-factly.

"I'm happy for you," replied Lucy, smiling and touching her mother on the shoulder.

"That's kind of you to say, dear," said Jean. "Thank you."

"Things with Aria and I have been going quite well, also," continued Lucy. "We're a thing now. We're together." She smiled over at Aria, and Aria smiled back.

"Well, that's just great!" beamed Jean. "I'm elated for the two of you. I sensed something was happening there, but I didn't want to interfere."

"I wish that this could be my Mom's reaction to this kind of news," said Aria. "But I expect snooty indifference mixed with sharp anti-gay comments."

"Oh, I'm sorry, dear," Jean bemoaned. "That's awful. I hope she comes around, for your sake. I can imagine it's very difficult to deal with such closed-mindedness."

"Yes," agreed Aria simply.

"Thank you, Mom," said Lucy. "I think we're going to head into my room and just talk for a little bit."

"Oh, well, all right," Jean replied, slowly nodding. Then an idea struck her. "Lucy, you still have Paul's card, don't you?"

"His business card?" asked Lucy inquisitively. "Yeah, I believe so."

"Can you please give his office a call soon?" pressed Jean. "He wants to speak with you."

Aria looked at Lucy with big eyes. It was the first she had heard of this.

"Yes, I will," Lucy said quickly. "Thank you."

Lucy began walking away from her mother, and Aria tagged along. Jean now wore a slightly perturbed expression.

"Please call him!" she called after the two as they left the hallway. Jean folded her arms.

SOME DAYS LATER, Aria was alone in her room sorting through some clothing on her bed. Her closet and dresser had been filled with things she no longer wore or cared for, and she had gotten it into her mind that it was time to do something about it. After folding and sorting the various items, she fed them into paper bags based on their type—shirts in this bag, pants in that bag—and slated them for donation. It felt good to downsize. It felt, in a way, as though she were exorcising her demons.

Aria was so enthralled by her task that she didn't notice her mother slinking into her room. Phyllis hung by the door for a moment and watched Aria put her clothes in the bags. It took a minute, but Aria finally looked up and caught eyes with Phyllis. But she didn't stop. Aria looked back down and continued her task.

"What are you doing?" Phyllis asked.

"I'm donating some clothes that I no longer wear," replied Aria. "It's all just taking up so much space."

"That's a good idea," offered Phyllis. "I don't imagine your next bedroom will have as much space as this."

Aria absorbed the comment and pressed on in her work.

"Have you given any thought to what you might like to do?"

"I don't know," Aria retorted.

"I think you really should," Phyllis continued. "I also think you should go through your father's things sooner rather than later. I've already called the estate sale company and we've scheduled them to come through in late January."

"What?" Aria snapped back incredulously. "That soon?"

"Aria, I have a lot of work to do on this house if I want to prepare it for sale by spring," said Phyllis. "We both have a lot of work to do."

"That's what I'm doing," Aria lobbed back, motioning toward the clothes.

"I've compiled a list of houses and condos that I'd like to show you," Phyllis went on. "I've picked a few here in Madeira if you'd like to stay local. I've also found some in the Royal Oak area if you'd like to be closer to the city. There are a lot of options, even in the winter."

Aria stopped, she tossed down the shirt she had in her hands onto the bed, and she sighed.

"Thank you," she said, exasperated. "I will take a look at them soon."

"I think I may be moving to Ann Arbor," Phyllis said. "I haven't decided yet, but I enjoy Ann Arbor and I've been pricing condos there. I would be happy to look for something for you there, as well."

"Enough!" Aria bleated. "I read you, loud and clear. I understand that you want me out of here. I will get out."

"Sweetie, it's not that—"

"No," countered Aria quickly. "I get it. Really."

"Hmph," intoned Phyllis, crossing her arms.

Aria just stood and stared at her mother for a few moments, feeling completely over it all. She hardly knew how to proceed so she just went with the first thing that came to her mind.

"My friend you met at Dad's funeral," Aria began. "Lucy. She's not just my friend. She's also my girlfriend. I'm gay, Mom. Okay? Now you know."

Phyllis paused, a look of confusion washing over her as she parsed Aria's words together.

"Well," said Phyllis after another moment of reflection. "Okay, then."

"You could support me, you know?" pressed Aria.

"Sweetie, I..." Phyllis began and then stopped. "Yes. You be you."

Now Aria crossed her arms, somewhat perplexed by her mother's response.

"What?"

"You be you, sweetie," repeated Phyllis. "That's fine. It was your father who wasn't a fan of the gays. He was from a different era. I've come to be indifferent. In fact, I find gay couples to more often than not be in better financial circumstances when they go to buy a house. Just six months ago I helped a nice lesbian couple purchase their dream home in Brighton. They were lovely to work with."

Aria took a deep breath, trying to piece together everything her mother was saying. She was caught off guard. This wasn't what she had expected.

"... thank you," said Aria.

Phyllis lifted a brow.

"Hmm," responded Phyllis with interest. "Well, I'll let you continue your project. Please let me know when you'd like to sit down and look at some of these homes I've found for you. I'm sure you'll like them."

"I will."

"Thank you, sweetie," Phyllis said in a tone conveying that she believed she'd won. With a smile, Phyllis turned and left Aria's room.

Aria, meanwhile, kept herself composed. She picked up the shirt she had thrown down, she folded it, and she tossed it into the appropriate bag. Her mind was all mixed up.

LUCY WAS DRESSED NICELY in slacks and a blouse, although she was also barefoot, sitting at the dining room table with her laptop open in front of her and her phone pressed to her ear. She had done her makeup and hair, and her face looked positive and bright as she spoke into the phone through a smile.

"Yes, thank you," she said in a chipper tone. "I appreciate that, Jenny. Yes, I will send you those references right after we get off of the phone. Your email is Jenny dot Reed at.... got it, yes. Thank you, sincerely."

Lucy paused, still smiling, and listened.

"Terrific," she went on. "Thanks, Jenny. Have a great day. Yes, goodbye."

Hanging up the phone, Lucy let out a deep exhale and slunk down in her seat. Putting on a performance for corporate HR was always a task, but it was a task she excelled at. The first phone interview had been a success. And after

Jenny called Lucy's references, she would then have to travel to New York for an in-person interview.

But it all felt so Herculean. Or maybe it was Sisyphean.

Lucy had a sour taste in her mouth as she composed the email she had promised Jenny. There was just something wrong about it all. Not that the job was out of her wheelhouse or that it wouldn't work out. In fact, it was exactly the kind of job that Lucy would be successful in. But things had changed. She had changed. And even after she hit send on the message and closed her laptop, Lucy felt deeply that she was going against what she truly wanted.

It was then that Jean walked into the room with a knowing look on her face. She paused and waited for Lucy to acknowledge her. Once Lucy felt her mother's presence, she looked up from her chair, half-smiled through flat lips, and shrugged.

"How did it go?" asked Jean.

"Great," said Lucy without enthusiasm.

Reaching into her pocket, Jean pulled out a small white business card. She handed it over to Lucy.

"Please," said Jean. "Call Paul. Do it now."

Lucy inspected the card for a moment in silence. Then she looked to her Mom, she smiled, and picked up her cell phone. With a satisfied smile on her own face, Jean turned and left the room once more.

Swiftly tapping the number into the screen, Lucy then raised the phone to her ear and waited as it rung.

"Paul Vonn's office," said a serious-sounding woman on the other end.

"Hi, I'm calling to speak with Mr. Vonn," said Lucy. "This is Lucy Burgess, and I believe he's expecting my call."

"Hold on, please," said the woman.

There was a pause, and Lucy waited, feeling her nerves rise up. Although she had met Paul before, and had a bit of a rapport with him, it was a much different proposition interacting with him in a more professional manner.

"Miss Burgess?" said the woman.

"Yes?"

"I'm transferring you to Mr. Vonn now," she said. "One moment."

There was another pause, and Lucy waited, psyching herself up and getting into her corporate character, just as she had done when talking to Jenny Reed. Shifting from her normal personality to this professional demeanor was like having some kind of spirit inhabit her body. It was so much different than her more casual personality at the coffee shop.

"Lucy," said Paul once he finally arrived on the phone. "I'm glad you called."

"Mr. Vonn," she replied with a hint of nervousness. "Paul, I mean."

"Yeah, Paul is fine," he offered with warmth. "I've been trying to get Jean to have you call me ever since our dinner some time ago. I'm guessing you've just been busy."

"Well, truth be told," Lucy admitted, breaking her character some. "I had been avoiding it."

"Avoiding it?" Paul repeated with concern. "Why is that?"

"You're... dating my Mom," said Lucy in earnest. "The entire situation is just... a little awkward."

"Yes, I do see how that could be the case," agreed Paul. "But, I assure you, my intentions are good. I've heard all the good things your mother has told me about you, your professional history, your skills and accomplishments, and I've taken them as the truth. You sound like the kind of person we could use here in Dearborn."

"That's kind of you to say," replied Lucy. "What is the position that you have available?"

"Assistant director of marketing and communications," said Paul. "You'd be responsible for enhancing the company's image and position within the marketplace and raising public awareness over all demographics. You'll work closely with the director of the department to establish a strategic direction for our marketing plan and increase visibility for our automotive products in the community. Does this sound like something you'd be interested in?"

"It does," admitted Lucy. "I do think it would be a good fit for my skill set and my professional interests."

"Obviously my say has a lot of pull," continued Paul. "You have my business card, correct?"

"I do."

"Please email me your resume and a cover letter, and I'll make sure it gets put into the correct hands," he advised. "This is a position we're hoping to fill in the new year. If you want to look further at the job description, it's on our website in the careers section."

"Okay," said Lucy. "I will do that. Both of those."

"That's great to hear," Paul said. "Thank you for calling, Lucy. I look forward to speaking with you further about this."

"Yes, thank you," Lucy replied. "Have a nice day, Paul."

"You do the same."

Lucy placed her phone down on the table. She flattened her lips as her mind raced. Now she had potentially two job offers. But the decision was much larger than just that.

CHAPTER 13

"*M*erry Christmas!" beamed Jean as Lucy sleepily sashayed into the kitchen, dressed in her pajamas. Lucy wiped at her eyes and smiled softly.

"Merry Christmas," she replied.

"I've got a quiche in the oven," Jean continued. "And I've got fancy coffee in the coffee pot. I picked it up from Fair Grounds the other day. Aria recommended it."

"All right," said Lucy. She wandered over to the coffee pot and poured herself a mug, topping it off with a splash of cream.

"I know we don't really do Christmas around here anymore," Jean offered. "But I still wanted to do something a little special. This is the first time you've been in this house on Christmas for at least a few years."

"That's true," Lucy agreed, now taking a sip of her coffee. "Thank you. The quiche smells amazing. What's in it?"

"Spinach, artichoke, and Swiss cheese," Jean said. "I found the recipe online."

"I can't believe how quickly Christmas snuck up," mused Lucy. "It's been such an odd year. It feels like time has flown by quickly, but also... this year kind of feels like the longest day of my life." She laughed to herself.

"I'm not sure I know what that means," Jean replied, furrowing her eyebrows.

"I just mean... time has actually moved quickly, but since this year has felt kind of lost to me, like I've taken a step back or a step outside of the life I had been living, it also feels like I'm stuck living the same day again and again."

"Like that Bill Murray movie?" asked Jean, trying to make sense of her daughter's words.

"Groundhog Day?" said Lucy. "No, not quite. Not literally. I just... nevermind," she said, waving the conversation off with a smile. "It doesn't matter. It's just been a strange year."

"Yes, I can agree with that," conferred Jean. She paused. "What is Aria doing today?"

"Nothing, I think," said Lucy. "We haven't really talked much about it. I know that her family hasn't really done anything special for Christmas for a while. And now that her Dad died, I think her Mom has just been pressuring her to organize the house and start clearing it out."

"Oh," Jean replied. "Did you get her a present?"

"A present? A Christmas present?"

"Yes, a Christmas present," reiterated Jean. "Did you get her something?"

"I... didn't," said Lucy, suddenly feeling guilty. "I guess it slipped my mind. Wow. How thoughtless, huh?"

"So I shouldn't expect a gift from you either, huh?" Jean teased.

Lucy made a face, and then took another sip of coffee.

"Well, I got you something," Jean went on. She reached for a small box sitting on the counter. Taking a few steps closer to Lucy, she handed the box over to her.

"Oh, Mom," said Lucy, her tone changing. "You really didn't have to. I'm sorry I didn't get you anything."

"It's all right," said Jean. "Go ahead and open it."

Lucy smiled softly, and looked down at the small box in her hand. She set her coffee mug down on the counter and began opening her Christmas present.

Underneath the wrapping paper was a textured black jewelry box. Lucy carefully popped the lid open and looked within. Inside was a thin gold chain attached to a small pendant with a diamond in it.

"What is this?" asked Lucy, removing the necklace from the box. She set the box down, unclasped the necklace, and began putting it around her neck.

"That was the very first piece of jewelry your father ever bought me," said Jean. "He got that for me our sopho-more year of college. He spent, well, pretty much all the money he had on that. I was looking through keepsakes last week, on the anniversary of his death, and I found that. I thought you might like to have it." Jean smiled gently.

"It's beautiful, Mom," said Lucy, looking down at the

necklace where it hung on her upper chest. "This is a very sweet gift. Thank you."

"It feels odd to be moving on from him, even after all these years," Jean went on. "Things with Paul are going well, and while I know I shouldn't feel guilty, I often do. But I know he would want me to be happy. It's just time for me to embrace this next stage of my life. Nothing lasts forever."

"That's true," Lucy agreed. "Nothing lasts forever." She thought about those words for a moment, looking down again at the necklace.

"If Aria is alone today on Christmas," said Jean. "You should probably go be with her."

"I should," Lucy confirmed. "Do you happen to have any other potential gifts lying around so I can pretend like I'm not a thoughtless girlfriend?" Jean chuckled.

"No, dear," said Jean. "But you could take her a piece of quiche."

WHEN LUCY DROVE up to Aria's house, she noticed Aria's car was backed in the driveway with the trunk open. A light snow fluttered down from the sky as Lucy parked at the curb. She stepped out of the car, holding a small container in her hand, and then walked up the driveway and looked around trying to spot Aria.

Soon enough, Aria came out from the front door of the house with a box in her arms. She smiled wide as soon as she saw Lucy.

"Merry Christmas!" said Aria as Lucy approached her.

"What are you doing?" Lucy asked in confusion. "Are you moving out? Merry Christmas."

"No, I'm not moving out," replied Aria with a grin. "This is just stuff I'm donating. I'm packing my car up today so that I can go drop it all off tomorrow morning."

"Oh," Lucy said, now following Aria as she carried the box over to her car and placed it in the trunk. "You've almost filled it."

"Yeah, this is a lot of junk," Aria agreed.

"Is any of this... your father's stuff?"

"No," Aria said. "I've been going through that stuff, plucking out things I want, and leaving the rest for the estate sale company to deal with. He had a lot of handy hobbies, and I don't know the first thing to do with any of that stuff. I wouldn't want to donate something that could be really valuable."

"This is for you," Lucy said, handing over the container she was holding. Aria accepted it and smiled.

"What is this?"

"It's a piece of quiche," replied Lucy. "From my Mom." Aria laughed.

"Thank you, Jean," she said.

"I, um... I didn't get you anything for Christmas," admitted Lucy sheepishly. "To be honest, Christmas hasn't been on my radar for a long time. And this year, it kind of snuck on me. It's been a rough year."

"Tell me about it," said Aria. "Well, have no fear. I'm not

upset that you didn't get me a gift. However, I did get you something."

"Well, damn it," Lucy said with an impish grin. Aria smiled back at her.

"I guess I'm done here," Aria surmised, then shutting the trunk of her car. "Come on, let's head inside so I can dig into this quiche."

Lucy nodded happily and followed as Aria let her into the house.

Sitting at the kitchen counter, Lucy had her second cup of coffee for the day. After a few sips, she set the mug down on a coaster on the countertop. Aria meanwhile hung near the microwave, and once the microwave sounded off with a series of beeps, she removed the plate from within and walked over to where Lucy sat with her now steaming hot piece of quiche.

"This looks amazing," said Aria. "All I had for breakfast was a croissant with jam. My Mom had picked up a few pastries yesterday. She left this morning for my aunt's house, her sister, to go celebrate Christmas with them. I told her I wasn't interested in going."

"I'm sorry, babe," replied Lucy with an empathetic expression. "You didn't want to go?"

"Not really," said Aria. "I'm sure it would just be a lot of pitiful expressions and condolences. My Mom gets a rise out of being the victim in circumstances like that. I'd rather just be alone."

"I can go if you want—"

"Yeah, get out," Aria teasingly said, and then laughed. "Stop. You know I don't mean you."

Lucy smiled.

"Is that necklace new?" asked Aria.

"This?" said Lucy, looking down and putting her fingers to the necklace. "Yes, my Mom gave it to me for Christmas. It was hers, the first jewelry gift my Dad ever gave her."

"That's sweet," Aria said, forking a piece of quiche into her mouth. She very quickly reopened her mouth and held her tongue out, making an expression of urgency. "Hot!"

"I can see the food in your mouth," quipped Lucy. "Just spit it out if it's too hot."

Aria muscled through the temperature of the quiche piece, chewing and swallowing. Then she put her fork down.

"I should give that a moment," she said, pushing the plate away slightly so she wouldn't get tempted.

"Yeah, don't injure yourself," Lucy pushed. "That tongue is an important part of our relationship."

Aria made a face, and then stuck out her tongue.

"So would you like to see my present to you?" asked Aria, wiping her hands now on a small towel. "I don't know if it's as good as your necklace, but it's something."

"Sure," confirmed Lucy with a reinvigorated smile. "I'll be happy to receive your gift."

Aria teasingly rolled her eyes, and then she stepped away from where Lucy sat and walked to the other end of the counter. There, near a small vase of flowers, was a manila folder. Aria picked the folder up and sauntered her way back over to Lucy, where Lucy looked on with an interested expression.

"Here," said Aria, handing the folder over to Lucy. Lucy accepted the folder, opened it up, and began looking through it.

"These are... house listings," Lucy responded, lifting a piece of paper out of a stack of a dozen or more.

"That's right," Aria confirmed. "That is a collection of houses that my Mom found for me based on some criteria I gave her."

"I'm not sure I understand how this is a gift for me..."

"Silly," said Aria. "I want you to help me choose. I want your input. Because I'm hoping that you will spend a lot of time with me in whatever house we choose together."

"Oh!" replied Lucy, finally getting it.

"It's not a diamond necklace," teased Aria. "But it is, you know, special."

"It is special," Lucy agreed with a touched smile. "Ooh! This one is nice." She handed a sheet back over to Aria.

"Yeah, I like this one, too," mused Aria, looking down into the page. "It's so cute and quaint."

"Most of these seem to be closer to Detroit," Lucy said. "Royal Oak, Berkley, Ferndale."

"There's a few in there for Madeira," countered Aria.

"Do you want to stay in Madeira?" asked Lucy. "Or are you thinking about leaving?"

"I don't know," said Aria. "I like it here, but I also feel like I've missed out on so much by staying here. I stayed in Madeira for my Dad. But now he's gone. And my Mom is talking about moving away, as well. I feel like maybe now is my time to flourish and try something new."

"Yeah, I get that," Lucy agreed. "Having grown up here, I wanted to leave as soon as I could. But I guess now, it's starting to grow on me."

"Do you think you want to stay in Madeira?" Aria wondered. "You've talked so much about missing New York. Honestly, I've been pretty worried that you might just disappear one day and go back."

"I won't disappear on you," Lucy said with a reassuring smile. "I'd never do that."

"So... what does that mean?"

"I guess I... I don't know," offered a confused Lucy. "I'm trying to figure it all out, still."

"What do you think of this one?" asked Aria, plucking a sheet from the folder and handing it over to Lucy. Lucy looked down into it for a moment.

"It's nice," mused Lucy. "It's not too big, but has a good amount of space. I like that it's all hardwood floors throughout."

"Me too," Aria agreed. She smiled at Lucy until Lucy looked back up to her. Then Lucy smiled again.

"When I lived in New York," Lucy began. "I never thought I would ever be able to afford to buy my own place. Forget about an actual house, even a condo in the neighborhoods I would want to live in were just so expensive. And I made good money, too! It was just too hard to save a down payment when you're paying that high rent along with your other bills. But this," she said, waving the paper. "This is a pretty little house for such a reasonable price. And Ferndale is a nice town."

"I can only afford to buy a house because of my inheritance and trust fund," replied Aria in earnest. "You may look at the price of this house here, compare it to New York prices, and think it's great. But other people I know who are around our ages, they'd look at this and think that it was just too expensive."

"I guess you're right," Lucy said.

"It's all relative," Aria went on. "But the thing that ties both situations together is the fact that, for young people, housing is so expensive. It's gotten out of hand. I mean, this house here isn't huge or uniquely special," she said, waving the paper. "But it's two-hundred and fifty thousand dollars. Quarter of a million dollars for this."

"Merry Christmas," Lucy teased. Aria couldn't help but chuckle.

"Right?" said Aria. "Anyway." She picked her fork back up and tried another bite of the quiche. It had cooled sufficiently and she could chew it without burning herself.

"I am thinking about staying," Lucy finally revealed. "But it's just a hard decision. It's hard because I have to admit to myself that that part of my life is over."

"It can be hard when you have to say goodbye to something before you're ready," Aria said knowingly. Lucy understood it immediately.

"Right," said Lucy.

Aria smiled as Lucy touched her hand. They both had

their problems to work on. But it felt good to have someone there to help get through it all.

LATER ON THAT NIGHT, alone in Aria's big house, the girls kissed and caressed one another in Aria's bed. On the nightstand next to the bed, a conical speaker released a chilled out, lazy tune with a beat, bordering on trip hop. And next to that speaker was a tall, thick candle, almost the same size as the speaker itself. The blanket only half covered their naked bodies, as the voracity with which they made out caused it to fall to the wayside. As Lucy rolled over and found herself on top of Aria, lips pressed together, she pushed her hand between Aria's legs and rubbed her fingers against Aria's wet flesh. Aria moaned into Lucy's mouth.

By the time the song playing faded into the next one, Lucy's face was between Aria's legs. With her nose resting on Aria's blonde bush, Lucy parted Aria's lips with her tongue, lapping in steady upward motions until she changed tactics and pursed her lips against Aria's clit, kisses that were each appointed with a firm suck. Aria put her hands on Lucy's head, little moans coming from her mouth with each breath, her legs spread and her knees lifted up slightly in the air. Her heart raced and she could feel the intensity build as Lucy pleasured her down below.

"That's nice," Aria intoned softly, her head falling to one side on the pillow. Her eyes were closed and her mouth hung half open, still offering up moans as she inhaled and exhaled.

Lucy's eyes darted upwards along Aria's body, and she watched as Aria's breasts rose and fell with her breathing. Aria's small belly inflated, too, and Lucy's eyes focused for a moment on a little birthmark that colored Aria's skin just south of her navel.

Soon, Aria began to twitch, her hips shifted sporadically and wiggled down into the sheet. Lucy didn't stop, and Aria's movements grew more severe until she started laughing and pushing herself off of Lucy. Lucy couldn't help herself, and she kissed Aria's pussy a couple more times before lifting her head up, and looking to Aria's face with a big grin.

"In the candle light," said Aria. "Your mouth and chin are glistening."

"Oh?" replied Lucy, wiping at her mouth with a small laugh. "Sorry. I blame you."

"Yeah, totally my fault for getting so wet," Aria lobbed back.

Lucy crawled up the length of Aria's body and collapsed down next to her, wrapping an arm around her middle. Aria, with her arm loosely around Lucy's neck, cuddled close.

"That was wonderful," mused Aria. The girls kissed delicately.

"I'm pretty good with my tongue, if I do say so myself," Lucy quipped. Aria laughed and kissed her again.

"In my dreams, we're both real adults who don't live at

home with our parents," Aria said longingly. "We have our own place together, and after sex I could just climb out of bed, and walk naked into the kitchen to get a glass of water. No sneaking around. Just freedom."

"I mean, your mother isn't here tonight," replied Lucy. "You could wander naked downstairs and get a glass of water if you wanted."

"Way to miss the point, Lucy," said Aria. They kissed once more.

"I'm teasing," Lucy admitted.

"I know you are." Another kiss.

"Well, I think your dream will be reality soon enough," said Lucy, her eyes expressing her adoration.

"I think you're right," agreed Aria. She hugged tighter to Lucy, and she threaded one of her legs between Lucy's. Then Aria and Lucy were kissing again, echoing their fervency from earlier. Before they knew it, they were back at it, kissing and laughing and touching one another in all the right places.

Their love went long into the night.

CHAPTER 14

The week between Christmas and New Year's Eve felt, as it always did, like everything was on pause. It was a week of reflection, and a time to question how one might want the next year to go. For Lucy, it was no different. In previous years, this week would have been spent recovering from the hangover of Christmas so that she was ready to go for New Year's Eve. But this year, Lucy had much more on her mind. It had been such a hard year, and she was eager for it to bloom into something much brighter for her.

But what would that mean? How would that look?

Coming out from her room with her laptop under her arm, Lucy saw her mother standing in the hallway in her coat and boots, primping in a mirror on the wall. Jean turned and saw Lucy coming her way, and she smiled.

"Paul's waiting for me in the driveway," said Jean. "We're about to head out to lunch. Would you like to join us?"

"I don't think so," said Lucy. "My brain's in overdrive. I feel like I've got so much to think about right now."

"Do you want to at least come out and say hello to him?" asked Jean, wrapping a scarf around her neck.

"I don't know..."

"Put on your shoes and come say hi," Jean pressed. "He'll be happy to see you."

"Yeah, okay," replied Lucy. She smiled.

Lucy and Jean walked out of the front door, one after another. Lucy had only stepped into her boots, and the laces trailed behind her. Her big winter coat hung open lazily, and underneath she wore a sweater and sweatpants. Together, mother and daughter approached the driver side window of Paul's large SUV. When he saw them come up, Paul lowered the window and smiled big.

"Lucy," he said jovially. "It's good to see you."

"Did you have a nice Christmas, Paul?"

"I did," he replied. "How about you?"

"Yeah, I did," she said.

"Thank you for sending your resume," Paul went on. "I think things are looking good. I spoke with HR and they'll be happy to bring you in for a interview in the new year. Do you think that will work for you?"

"Yeah, I think so," Lucy agreed. Jean was looking at her with a motherly smile, and when Lucy caught her looking, she smiled back.

"Terrific," Paul said. "I will not be at the interview, but they are aware of our relationship. I'm sure I don't have to tell you to do your best and be professional, but I assure you that there's no reason to be nervous. So long as you meet the requirements that HR has laid out and you present well, I believe the job is yours."

"Thank you, Paul," replied Lucy. "That's very reassuring to hear you say."

"Isn't he great?" Jean interjected with affection for her beau. She stood grinning for a moment. "It's getting cold. I'm going to get in the car. You have a great afternoon, dear."

Jean leaned in and embraced Lucy tightly, and Lucy warmly returned the gesture.

"Thanks," said Lucy. "You two have a nice lunch."

"We shall," said Paul.

Jean rushed around to the other side of the car and got in. After she got situated and put on her seat belt, both she and Paul bid Lucy farewell, and they reversed out of the driveway and onto Elm. Jean waved at Lucy through the window, Lucy waved back, and then the car rolled away. Lucy stood there for a moment, watching and smiling. It was then that a firm decision struck her.

Lucy changed out of her sweats and into something more appropriate to go out in, jeans, a loose cowl-neck sweater, nice leather boots, and her winter coat. She felt good, relaxed, and truly happy. As she walked down the sidewalk on Elm Street, a light flurry of snow fluttering from the sky, she felt peace in a way that she hadn't felt for a very long time. The year had dealt her a bad hand, but she was pushing through it. It felt good to be getting through the muck and mire and to finally feel like things were going her way.

She made her way downtown, a blithe smile on her face. The old Lucy had never been happy to be downtown in Madeira during any of her rare visits home. But Madeira had changed, and Lucy had changed as well. No longer did she feel she needed the supposed excitement of the big city. It never really was all that was promised. Her old life in New York City, now that she looked back on it with a renewed vision, had been a struggle. It had been a lot of sacrifice for little gain. Things were calmer here in Madeira, slower, and infinitely easier.

When Lucy opened the door to the coffee shop, a wave of warm air hit her cold face and comforted her. Behind the counter were both Aria and Wendy, and as they saw Lucy enter, they both smiled and said their greetings.

"Look who it is," mused Aria happily, crossing her arms and looking across the counter at her girlfriend. Her adoring expression said everything that needed to be said about her feelings for Lucy.

"It's me!" replied Lucy with a chuckle. "I'm here."

"Welcome!" said Aria. "Can I interest you in a dirty chai latte?"

"I think that sounds wonderful," Lucy agreed. She unzipped her coat and shoved her gloves into her pockets. "Thank you."

"Large dirty chai latte," Aria said to Wendy. Wendy gave her a thumbs up and began making Lucy's drink.

"Hey," said Lucy, now leaning over the counter and giving Aria a kiss. Aria returned the kiss gleefully.

"Hey," she replied.

"I've got some news," Lucy conferred. "Big news, I think."

"Oh, big news," repeated Aria. "I'm all ears."

"I'm going to take the job," admitted Lucy. "With Paul, at the auto company. I mean, I still have to do the interview, but I think it's inevitable. Paul said as much."

"Wow, so this means... you're staying in Michigan," Aria clarified. "You're not going back to New York?"

"I think that's what it means," said Lucy with a growing smile. "I figured, I didn't get you a Christmas gift, so maybe this will make up for it." Aria laughed.

"Yeah, I'd say that this makes up for it," Aria beamed happily. "I'm really just floored by this news," she went on, putting her hands on her cheeks. "Am I smiling too big?" Now Lucy laughed.

"No, you're smiling the appropriate amount," quipped Lucy. "I've just been thinking so hard about all this for so long, and today when I saw Paul and he told me that the job was basically mine if I wanted it, it really made me think about what I truly want out of my life. And since being back here in Madeira, my priorities have changed so much. Now that you're in my life, I just couldn't imagine leaving you or leaving this thing we have together. It's been a shining light in a dark time of my life."

"I feel the same way," replied Aria. She gripped tightly to Lucy's hand.

"I'm sorry to interrupt," said Wendy, moving into the conversation. "But your dirty chai is ready, lady."

"Thank you," said Lucy, giving her manager a smile. Then Lucy realized what she had to do. "Oh... Wendy."

"Yes?"

"I... um," Lucy began. "There's a very good chance that I'll be getting a new job within a few weeks or so. At one of the Big Three, working in marketing and communications. You know, my career area..."

"Right," said Wendy with a knowing nod. "That's fine, Lucy. I completely understand. I knew you were just here riding out the down economy, and that's okay. It was inevitable that you'd move on. I'm happy for you." She smiled in earnest.

"That's very understanding of you," said Lucy. "I appreciate it. And I appreciate this," she said, taking up her cup of coffee.

"No problem," said Wendy. "And that's on me. You're still coming in for your scheduled shifts over the next couple weeks, right?"

"Oh, absolutely," Lucy confirmed. "I wouldn't do that to you."

"Great," said Wendy. She smiled once again. "I hope the new job works out and you get back to where you want to be."

"I think I'm already there," said Lucy. Her eyes moved to Aria, and they grinned at each other. Never before had Lucy felt her life was moving in the precise direction that it should be. There were always hiccups, or the goalposts kept moving, or things would be right once this or that happened. But those kind of feelings had subsided. She knew that this was right. She knew that, for all of her ups and downs, her old life blowing up and forcing her to move home, this path was the one she was supposed to be on.

Aria felt it, too. They had both had a circuitous ride. But it was worth it for what their future had in store. That was abundantly clear.

BACK AT HOME, Lucy sat crosslegged on the couch with her computer perched in her lap. She swiftly typed into the keyboard, composing a message, the words coming to her quickly. It was a professional message of gratitude, but it was short and to the point. She wanted them to know that she was thankful for the opportunity, but it just wasn't going to work out. After writing the message, Lucy read it over a few times for errors, she made a couple minor changes, and then she took a deep breath and hit send.

And that was the real end of a chapter in her life. She had once thought of herself as very cosmopolitan. She had this image of herself in her mind, an image of a young professional, successful, important, a real career woman. This image had really taken shape in Lucy's mind less than a decade prior, around the time she was the same age as Aria, when she got her first big promotion at work. The money was nice, the responsibility made her feel important, but it was the title that did it to her. No longer would she tell people she was an assistant. She had become an account manager, and she was working with important people.

But it was all just a mirage. It was a story she told herself to make her feel like she had made it. The truth was, she had always been struggling inside. She couldn't make a relationship last, she was a long distance away from her family, and her life was just the product of putting too much stock in what she had seen in movies and on television. This was all clear to Lucy now as she sat on her mother's couch, ruminating about where her life might go next.

Then her phone rang. It was Lorna.

"Hello?" Lucy answered with a wistful smile.

"Lucy, it's Lorna," she said. "Jenny just called and told me you turned down the in-preson interview. What's the deal?"

"Yeah," Lucy admitted. "I turned it down. I'm not going to be coming back to New York, Lorna."

"Are you serious?" Lorna boomed incredulously. "Why not?"

"You know, I just don't think it's right for me anymore," Lucy went on. "I thought I missed it in the beginning, but after some time here in Michigan, I've realized that the things I thought I loved about New York just aren't... lovable."

"I don't think I understand," said Lorna. "You don't care about the nightlife, or the opportunities, the great food, the shopping? You don't care about being in the center of everything, or working for a company that really has an effect on all of American culture? You don't care about being in the greatest city in the world?"

"I guess I don't," Lucy said plainly. "For all of that stuff, I was still unhappy there at my core. I thought I had what I always wanted, but being back home has shown me that New York wasn't the answer."

"I am just so surprised," Lorna conferred with a hint of sadness in her voice. "You sound like a totally different Lucy than the woman I knew before."

"Maybe I am," said Lucy. "But look, I do want you to know how appreciative I am that you reached out to me with the opportunity, Lorna. That means a lot to me. But I think this next stage of my life is going to be here in Michigan. I've reconnected with my Mom, I've got a great job opportunity on the horizon, and honestly... I've met the girl of my dreams. I can't leave all this now."

Lorna paused in their conversation, taking in all that Lucy was saying.

"I get it," she said after a moment. "That makes a lot of sense, Lucy. Well, I'm sorry it didn't work out but I wish you well in your new life."

"Lorna, thank you," Lucy replied. "I'm really starting to feel happy, and I know it's different because this isn't a feeling I've felt in a long time."

"That's good to hear," said Lorna. "Well, I should get back to work. Take care, Lucy."

"You too, Lorna," she said. "Take care."

"Goodbye," said Lorna.

"Goodbye," said Lucy.

When Lucy hung up, it felt final. Although Lorna had been a good work friend in her old life, it didn't feel like a real friendship that would carry on. And that was okay. People come and go. That's just life. Lucy smiled softly, cradling her phone in her hands for a minute or two as she continued to reflect on how this was all playing out.

Then she heard the front door open up.

Jean came in through the door, and she kicked the snow off of her boots on the door frame. She began taking off her winter gear, and as she did this she looked up.

"Lucy?" she called out.

"I'm here," replied Lucy from the living room.

Jean smiled to herself, finished removing her coat, and hung it up on the coat rack. Then, in her socks, she rounded the corner from the small foyer and entered the living room. There she saw Lucy, still sitting crosslegged on the couch with her laptop.

"At least you're dressed now," Jean joked. Lucy chuckled.

"I went out and came back already," Lucy said. "I got a coffee from Fair Grounds."

"That's nice, dear," said Jean. "I'm surprised I didn't see you downtown, then. Paul and I got lunch at Fratelli's. They serve such large portions there. I couldn't finish my eggplant parmesan. It's ridiculous." Lucy laughed again.

"Well, you're a small lady," Lucy said. "I'm sure other people could finish it."

"Paul couldn't finish his lunch, either," countered Lucy.

"And he had the steak. Just too much food. I guess it's how they justify their prices."

Lucy smiled and shook her head.

"You look pretty happy today," Jean noted. "It's nice to see you in better spirits."

"Yeah, I just feel... good today," replied Lucy, still smiling. "It's a good day."

"That's nice to hear," said Jean.

"I've decided that I'm going to stay," Lucy admitted firmly. "I'm going to stay in Michigan."

"What? That's wonderful, dear," Jean beamed. "I'm so happy to hear that. I know you were feeling torn with that job in New York, but things have been going so good for you here lately. I'm glad you're seeing it the same way."

"Yeah," said Lucy. "I'm glad I'm finally seeing it, too."

"I think this calls for some celebration," Jean declared. "I've got this very nice bottle of port wine that Paul gave me some time ago. I'll go pour us two little glasses and we can toast to you being back in Michigan for good."

"All right, great," Lucy said. Jean smiled blithely at her daughter, lifted a single finger up, and then she scurried off into the kitchen.

Lucy was still smiling, too. She closed her laptop and set it aside. Then she popped up from the couch and walked over to the window. The snow painted a beautiful winter scene outside. Lucy was back home.

ARIA SAUNTERED into her house after her shift at the coffee shop. She put the cup of coffee she carried in on a small table near the door, and she stepped out of her snowy boots. Next she removed her coat, and walked it over to a closet. After her coat was hung, she placed her boots in the closet as well, and then she grabbed her coffee and continued on her merry way.

Passing through the kitchen, Aria ended up the the sitting room in the back of the house, the room that had once been occupied by her father. She was used to coming home from work, whipping up some lunch and serving it to him amid an often too-loud television. But for the past few weeks it had been quiet. The room hadn't changed much. His chair was still there. But he was gone.

She felt sad standing there, remembering how it used to be. But there was also a keen sense of liberation. Before, Aria would often try to rush home for fear that her father was hungry. Now, however, there was no need to rush. After work, she had stuck around for a half hour chatting with Wendy and Adam. The coffee she carried was her second cup. It never would have been like that before.

Aria knew she had to push on, however. This was a time she knew was coming in her life, she just didn't know when it would come. And now that it was here, she knew she must make the most of it. Most of her twenties had been sacrificed in service to her father's illness. But she was still young. There was so much future in front of her, a future she could live on her own terms.

Turning from the room, Aria began moving into the

kitchen but she stopped when she heard someone descending the stairs in the front of the house. She hung near the kitchen entrance and waited, sipping on her coffee, until her mother reached the bottom of the stairs, turned, and came waltzing down the hallway toward her.

"Aria," said Phyllis. "There you are."

"Hey," replied Aria nonchalantly.

"Listen, I have a few items to update you on," continued Phyllis as she drew closer.

"Okay," said Aria. "I'm listening."

"First, I've decided that I'm going to fly down to Cape Coral to spend New Year's with my cousin Betty in Florida," Phyllis asserted. "I'm leaving tomorrow."

"Oh," Aria intoned. "Well, all right. Have fun."

"I will," said Phyllis without missing a beat. "I'll be gone for a week, and I hope in that time you can be finished in sorting through your father's personal belongings, as our appointment with the estate sale company has been bumped up to the second weekend in January."

"Okay," agreed Aria. "I can do that. I think I'll just leave much of it to them, anyway."

"That sounds fine, sweetie," replied Phyllis with an air of near-indifference. "But what I'd really love for you to do is give me some more definite direction on your possible housing needs going forward. Did anything in that folder look good to you?"

"Yeah," said Aria. "It was a good selection of houses. I have been thinking about it, and I think to balance out location and price, I'd like to focus in on listings in Ferndale."

"That's wonderful," Phyllis conferred. "While I'm down in Florida, I'll hit up the MLS and search for some more options. You can look at the various retail housing sites, too, though I'll have access to homes that have yet to arrive on the market."

"Okay," said Aria. "Thank you."

"I'll be sure to email you a list of potentials as soon as I can," continued Phyllis. "We'll want to get the ball rolling quickly so that you don't miss out on the home of your dreams." She snapped her fingers.

"Sure."

"Perfect," Phyllis beamed. "I'm on my way out to Kelly's house for a little get-together with the girls. Don't wait for me for dinner. I expect to be out a bit late."

"Have a good time," Aria said, making sure to hide her sarcasm as best as she could.

"Thank you, Aria," Phyllis replied. "You do the same, sweetie."

With that, Phyllis sped off. Aria sipped her coffee and watched her mother until the door closed behind her.

CHAPTER 15

It was early on in the evening of New Year's Eve, and Lucy and Aria were together on the floor in the sitting room at Aria's house. Lucy had a glass of red wine, and Aria had a wine glass with sparkling water in it. They sat opposite one another with a cardboard box between then. Lucy took a sip of her wine as Aria pulled something out of it.

"Wow," remarked Lucy, watching as Aria exhumed what looked to be a large metal telephone handset. "What in the heck is that?"

"It's a radio," replied Aria. "Like a walkie talkie, I guess, but I don't think it necessarily communicated with another like it. I think my Dad said it was used to radio the base or something in the war. I might be wrong, though."

"It's... so big," said Lucy. She accepted the handset as Aria handed it over. Lucy put it to her ear and smiled.

"Breaker, breaker, one nine. Isn't that what they say? I think I heard that in a movie." Aria laughed softly.

"You know, I really have no idea," she said.

"Sorry," replied Lucy, suddenly feeling embarrassed. She took the handset down from her ear. "I didn't mean to joke about war or anything."

"It's okay," offered Aria empathically. She accepted the the handset back from Lucy and replaced it in the box. "Oh, check this out!"

"Is that an... ashtray?" asked Lucy, watching as Aria removed the small silver ashtray from the box.

"Yeah, it is," said Aria, now passing it over to Lucy."It was some kind of employee gift that my Dad got at his first job in the auto industry. He worked at Hudson, an old car company that doesn't exist anymore. This was when he was in his late teens, I think, before the Korean War and before he got into engineering. I think he worked in the factory back then, but I'm not sure what he did specifically."

"It's a cool little piece," Lucy admitted, flipping the ashtray around and looking at it from a few angles. "But you don't smoke."

"I could use it as a little change dish or something," Aria proposed with a shrug. "I think it's neat, with the Hudson logo engraved on it. I tried to look it up and couldn't find anything about it."

"Nice," Lucy responded with a smile. She handed it back to Aria and then took another drink.

"He's got a lot of cool stuff but I don't know what I'd do with most of it," Aria went on. "When I look through it, I just want to keep it all. But that's just me missing him. I know the stuff isn't him. It's just stuff. He's still there in my memories."

Lucy smiled and nodded, and she reached out and delicately placed her hand on Aria's knee for support.

"And it's like, how many hammers do I really need?" quipped Aria with a small laugh. Lucy laughed with her.

"Right," agreed Lucy. "But if he does have some decent tools, you should probably take them. They'd definitely come in handy when you have a place of your own."

"That's true," said Aria. "I've gotten so used to just calling my parents' friend Fred when we need something done around here. He's a handyman that's helped us out ever since my Dad got sick."

"Well, grab a hammer or two and a drill," Lucy goaded. "And whatever else looks like something we might use."

"We?" said Aria quickly, her eyes lighting up and her smile curving into a smirk.

"You," corrected Lucy, obviously teasing with her tone and expression. "I definitely meant you. I can wield a hammer to hang up picture frames, but that's the extent of my tooling abilities." Aria laughed once again.

"Okay, I'll make sure to grab the nicest looking pieces I can," Aria confirmed. "So that I can use them whenever the time comes. Which reminds me. My Mom has already sent me another list of houses from Florida. That woman doesn't stop. Lucy, she wants me out and she wants me out now." Lucy grinned.

"Does it piss you off at all?" she asked. "I mean, I know

you take it in stride and make jokes about it, but does it hurt you that she's so pushy?"

"Ah... no," Aria said with certainty. "I know who she is. I know she doesn't want to be here or deal with this big house anymore. And honestly, I feel the same way. I don't have the desire to manage this place. It was one thing when my Dad was still here, but now it's just a big pile of work that neither of us want. I want to break free as much as my Mom does."

"Yeah, I understand," said Lucy. "Do you think you'll take any furniture with you?" She motioned to the furniture around them in the room.

"No," said Aria. "It's not really my aesthetic. I've never really had the kind of freedom you get as a real functioning adult with your own living space. I'm looking forward to starting fresh."

"Well..." began Lucy, somewhat sheepishly. "You know I've got this storage unit in Brooklyn that I have to deal with. It's full of my furniture. It's mostly mid-century modern type stuff. I have some pictures on my phone if you want to look. Maybe you might like some of that."

"Hmm, that's an interesting thought," said Aria, a smiling growing across her lips. "Knowing you, it's probably pretty nice furniture."

"It is," agreed Lucy. "That's why I kept it and have been paying rent every month on that damn unit. I'm ready to kill that bill." Aria laughed.

"So what's the plan with all that stuff then?" questioned Aria.

"I'll probably just have to pay to ship it all out here now,"

Lucy said, waving it off with a sigh. "Whatever. I'll deal with it the new year. But! It is nice furniture and I think you should take a look at it."

"I definitely will," agreed Aria. Her smile was happy and genuine. It was obvious what they had together was the real deal. It was a palpable feeling.

Lucy hoisted herself up from the floor and made a kissy face at Aria. Aria returned the gesture with glee, and she watched as Lucy turned from her and trotted off toward the kitchen with her empty wine glass aloft. Aria's eyes watched Lucy's butt move in her tight leggings, and she felt passion in her heart. It felt as though it happened so quickly, but this was love. This was the kind of relationship she had always hoped for herself. This was something big and this was something special.

After a quick moment or two, Lucy returned from the kitchen, her glass refilled with red, and Lucy caught Aria gazing at her with a dreamy expression on her face. Lucy smiled and raised a brow, intrigued and amused by how her girlfriend looked at her.

"Hey," said Lucy, standing there just a few feet away. "Are you okay?"

"Lucy, I love you," said Aria with a full, open heart and a smile. "I'm really happy I met you."

"I love you, too," replied Lucy blithely, feeling the warmth in the room. "I don't know if I would have survived Madeira without you."

Lucy let out a small chuckle with her words, but her big smile slowly lead to a tear coming from her eye. It was then that she knew for absolute certain she had made the right decision in staying.

"Are you okay?" asked Aria.

"I'm more than okay," replied Lucy. "I'm perfect."

LATER ON THAT NIGHT, the girls debated whether or not they should watch the New Year's Even festivities on television. Lucy had actually been in Times Square a couple of times to celebrate, and her summery of the event was that it was kind of a let down and the crowd could be suffocating. Aria's opinion was that the happiness and pomp on TV always felt so fake. In the end, they decided that neither of them really cared to watch and would instead just rather listen to music and spend the time with each other.

By the time midnight rolled around, the two were rolling around in Aria's bed, gleefully exploring one another, sharing soft kisses, and letting their bodies do the celebrating for them. It was certainly a pleasurable way to ring in the new year.

When Lucy woke up the next morning, she found herself alone in Aria's bed. She stretched her arms above her head and yawned, sleepily looking around and wondering where her lover had gone off to. As the new day —and the new year—dawned on her, Lucy crawled out of bed and wiped at her eyes as they adjusted to the light coming in from the large window on the opposite side of the room. She was fully nude, but she didn't feel exposed at all. Lucy felt comfortable and happy.

She found her black underwear on the floor at the foot of the bed, and she lazily put them on, stumbling slightly as the leghole got caught on one of her feet. Lucy chuckled at her clumsiness as she righted herself and continued getting dressed. Instead of getting back into her clothes from the night before, Lucy instead wandered over to the sofa and dug through a canvas bag she had brought with her. From the bag she pulled a soft purple long-sleeve shirt and a pair of plaid cotton shorts, her presumed sleeping attire that was of no use the night before. Lucy put on her clothes and then she pressed on, ambling toward the door and making her way downstairs.

As she walked down the staircase to the main floor, her nose was tickled by a very enticing scent. Lucy inhaled deeply, smiled, and suddenly realized how hungry she was. The smell in the air had hints of garlic and rosemary, and it inspired Lucy to pick up her pace and get into the kitchen to see what was happening. Upon rounding the corner and entering the kitchen, she saw the backside of Aria, dressed in a gray hoodie and patterned lounge pants, standing in front of the stove, sizzle and steam rising up in front of her.

"That smells wonderful," offered Lucy, walking through the kitchen and toward Aria. Aria turned from her work and smiled big when she saw Lucy.

"Well, thank you," replied Aria with a sparkle in her eye. She turned back to the stove, sticking her spatula into a cast iron skillet of cubed potatoes. Meanwhile, Lucy slipped behind her, wrapped her arms around Aria's waist, and hugged her from behind, punctuating her affection with a kiss on Aria's neck.

"I'm really hungry now," admitted Lucy, looking at the food. "What all do we have going on here?"

"Potatoes, fried up in butter with some rosemary," said Aria, pointing with her spatula. "And over here, I've got the fixings for an omelet. I'm going to make a French omelet."

"Ooh!" Lucy gushed. "I love French omelets. I've never been able to successfully pull one off, though. I always end up burning it."

"Yeah, it's a bit delicate," admitted Aria. "But I'm pretty decent at it."

"I can't wait to eat it," replied Lucy happily, giving Aria's waist another squeeze. "I love you," she said. Lucy enjoyed how those words sounded coming out of her mouth.

"I love you, too," Aria agreed. She was glowing.

Once breakfast was made and ready to eat, the girls sat down at the the kitchen table and dug in. A carafe of coffee sat between them, and they each had full mugs. The morning light shone in from the sliding glass door near the table, along with a shimmering glare from the bright white snow in the backyard. It was a new year, and everything felt calm, relaxed, easy, and fresh.

"Do you have any resolutions for the new year?" Aria asked, then forking a potato chunk into her mouth and chewing.

"Normally I spend December thinking about my resolutions," said Lucy. "Spend the first two weeks of January all gung ho, and then I give up and go back to my old ways. But this past year, I don't know, it felt like the whole thing was an exercise in getting my resolutions right."

"Okay," Aria offered with a small smile. "What do you think you got right in this last year?"

"Well, I don't mean to brag," Lucy began, giving Aria a knowing laugh. "But one of the things I'm most proud of is that I lost seven pounds. That's a lot on a small framed woman like me. I was running when the weather was nice, I drank a lot less booze this year, and because I was living at home and not living it up in New York, I wasn't going out to eat as much. At all, really. It's a huge accomplishment for me."

"Absolutely," Aria happily agreed. "I'm proud of you. I think that's just awesome, Lucy. Anything else you feel accomplished about?"

"I feel accomplished that I was able to come to the decision to stay in Michigan," Lucy continued. "For a moment, it felt I was, in a way, giving up a dream I always had. But that's not it at all. I think I just reached a point in life where the excitement of the city just isn't a draw to me anymore. I'm getting so old." Lucy's voice conveyed lament, but Aria just laughed.

"Lucy," she teasingly chastised. "You're thirty-five. That's not old."

"Well, sometimes I feel old," countered Lucy. "I'm older than you. I'm old enough to realize living the city party girl life isn't my thing anymore."

"It's just a new era for you," Aria said. "That's all it is."

"Yeah," Lucy begrudgingly agreed. "I mean, I know you're right. Still, it was a really hard decision for me. I still feel a bit like I'm giving up a dream. Just a little."

"You can always go back and visit if you want," said Aria. "And besides, Detroit isn't that bad. There are some great restaurants downtown. There's plenty of music. There's some theater. I'm guessing it's been a while since you spent any time in Detroit. And if we're living in Ferndale, we'll be so much closer to the city."

"What are you proposing?" Lucy asked wryly, a smirk painted on her face. Aria laughed.

"I don't know just yet," said Aria, slicing a bite off of her omelet with a fork. "I still have to find a house."

"What are you going to do about Fair Grounds?" Lucy posited.

"I don't know," said Aria, sticking the fork in her mouth and then chewing. After she swallowed, she spoke again. "Quit, I guess."

"And then what are you going to do?"

"I've got some ideas brewing," admitted Aria. "One thing at a time."

"So, then, what are your resolutions for the new year?" Lucy lobbed back. "Or, your proud accomplishments of this past year?"

"I'm doing resolutions," asserted Aria. "And this year, I'm going to live for me. I've been selfless for too long and it's time that I got a little selfish. You know, in a good way."

"Yeah, definitely," Lucy agreed, continuing into her breakfast as she listened.

"I'm going to do this house thing and I'm going to find the place that suits me best," Aria went on. "I'm going to figure out a career and I'm going to just go for it. I feel like this year is going to be my year."

Lucy smiled and replied with a slow nod.

"And most of all, what I'm looking forward to," said Aria. "Is being a strong, confident, out, lesbian woman. It's been so hard, especially these last few years living here at home, having to neglect my feelings and hide away and feel kind of... shameful, you know? I can't do that anymore. I need to be myself and live my best life."

"And I think that's amazing," confirmed Lucy. "I think you're right on the money. I'm so happy for you, Aria. I think you're going to really enjoy living your life by your own rules. I've always known you to be a positive and good person. You've already got all that down. This is just going to make you an unstoppable force."

"You know, you told me last night that you didn't think you could have made in Madeira without me," said Aria. "But I don't think I could have reached this point, feeling comfortable in my skin, being able to come out to my Mom, growing into a more self-assured woman, I don't think I could have done it without you. You're a real inspirational woman, Lucy. You're the kind of woman who just goes for it. And that's who I want to be going forward."

"We're a good pair," Lucy confided with both authority and glee.

Her words were obvious and the feeling was mutual. Lucy and Aria had experienced tough times, but they had found each other at just the right moment and it had been a boon for them both. Now, with a new year on the horizon, they both had refreshed outlooks on life and on love. There was so much ahead of them, and it felt comforting to know that they would face it together.

LUCY PULLED into the driveway of her own house, a bemused smile plastered on her face. She was happy and excited. She imagined what life was going to be like for her this year, and how everything was looking up. She thought about her new job and how that might go, and she even dreamed about what car she might buy for herself once she started getting paid again. Driving her Mom's car, a reliable but small SUV, had worked out all right, but Lucy imagined herself in something a lot sportier. Something red with a sunroof, maybe.

She had been lucky that her Mom had been getting chauffeured around by Paul so much lately. But for Lucy to have her own car would be the freedom she so desperately craved.

After grabbing her overnight bag from the backseat of the car, Lucy slammed the door and walked up the pathway to the front door. She was feeling good, and even bounced a little as she walked. It was a clear day, a blue sky, and the sun was shining. Sticking her key into the door, she opened it up and waltzed in feeling a song in her heart.

"I'm so over the moon!" she heard her mother explain upon walking in. "I'm just flabbergasted."

Lucy raised an eyebrow and looked around for her Mom. Jean stepped into view down the short hallway near the kitchen, and when she saw Lucy standing there, her face brightened.

"Let me call you back, Susan," said Jean into her phone. "Lucy just came home. Thank you so much. I love you, too. Yes, me too. Goodbye!"

Jean lowered her phone from her ear and spread her arms out. The excitement on her face was apparent. It was the most excited Lucy had seen her mother in a very long time, as Jean was usually more of a reserved woman.

"What's going on?" Lucy asked, stepping out of her boots and walking further into the house.

"Lucy," said Jean. "Paul asked me to marry him last night."

"Are you serious?"

"I'm serious!" Jean beamed.

"Mom..." said Lucy, moving toward her. "That's amazing. I'm so happy for you!" She approached Jean and hugged her tightly, and Jean eagerly hugged Lucy back.

"It's incredible!" Jean beamed, now stepping back from their embrace. She stuck her hand forward and showed Lucy the ring. It was big.

"Wow," Lucy replied, taking hold of her mother's hand to better look at it. "That is some ring. Isn't this all a little sudden, though?"

"I have something to tell you," Jean pivoted. "Paul and I

have been seeing each other a little longer than I told you. We met last January, almost a year ago. I was cagey about it because I felt a bit guilty and worried what you might think."

"Mom," said Lucy plainly. "As long as you're happy, I'm happy. I think it's wonderful. I'm really happy for you. And that ring, it's beautiful."

"I know," said Jean, her wild happiness returning, looking down once more at her ring. "I can't believe it. I just... I never thought I'd find love again. My face feels hot. Do I look red?" Jean put her hands to her face to feel herself and Lucy laughed.

"You look fine," she confirmed.

"It doesn't feel real," Jean went on. "It feels like a dream."

"That's so great, Mom," Lucy said. "You deserve it."

"Thank you, dear," Jean said, stepping closer for yet another hug. Lucy squeezed her tight.

It was going to be a great year. As Lucy hugged her mother in celebration of her engagement, her mind drifted to thoughts of Aria and their growing love. She imagined a ring on her own finger one day. Maybe that would come. Regardless of what her future held, Lucy was elated that she was here in Madeira, here with her Mom, and most of all that she had been here to meet Aria. This stumble she had taken in life had at first seemed like the end of her good times. But it was obvious now that that notion was the farthest thing from Lucy's reality.

The good times were only just beginning.

CHAPTER 16

EPILOGUE

*D*ressed in a breezy white blouse and a pair of blue linen shorts, Aria floated into her living room with a vase of lilies in her hands. Her hair was tied back with a handkerchief and her black glasses were sliding down her nose, her bare feet stepped lightly on the wood floor below. She had a content smile on her face as she walked the flowers over to the coffee table, set them in the middle of it, and then adjusted the flowers once more so that they hung just so.

The living room was small and quaint, with wood trim around the windows and door frames. There was a brick fireplace on one wall, painted white, that had been retrofitted with a gas burner inside of it. On the mantle above the fireplace there were various trinkets and decorative items, as well as another vase of flowers. The furniture in the room was mid-century modern, as was the couch with its dark blue upholstery and smooth, stem-like legs. It was a curated room that looked lived-in and cozy. Aria put her hands on her hips, looked around the room, and smiled to herself.

She then sat down on the couch and leaned forward to the coffee table upon which her laptop sat. She opened the computer and the screen came to life. This had been a routine all day, checking the computer for an email or checking her phone for an email, and she could only divert herself from her anxious checking by cleaning and organizing the house. It was all she could do to stay sane.

Outside it was a sunny afternoon in mid summer. The windows were open and a nice, cool breeze wafted into the house, sometimes causing the curtains to dance and spin. Everything felt light and easy. Apart from Aria's nervousness. But it was a good kind of nervousness. In her heart, she knew the news would be good. She just had to wait for the certainty of that feeling, though.

She loaded up her email and looked for new messages. Nothing. She sighed and shut the laptop quickly with a hint of disappointment. Looking around the room, Aria knew she was finished with all the cleaning she could do. But she needed to get her hands on something to take her mind off of checking her email. Pushing herself up from the couch, Aria flitted quickly into the kitchen.

The kitchen was tight, but there was enough room to move around. The appliances were stainless steel, and the countertops were butcher block. Above, the white cabinetry brought it all together. Everything about the house was cute, well-maintained, purposeful. When Aria had purchased the house, it needed little work, and she was happy about that. The previous owners had made it nice for her. Aria was happy to finally have her own slice of freedom. This home felt like relief.

From the refrigerator she plucked out some heirloom tomatoes, a jalapeño, a bundle of cilantro, a plump shallot, a lime, and a yellow bell pepper. After splaying it all out on the counter, she grabbed a medium glass bowl from the cabinet above her and began her task. She started by cutting up the shallot right on the butcher block, using her large chef's knife to then corral the chopped bits and feed them into the bowl. Aria flicked a bit of salt into the bowl, and then she proceed on to the tomatoes.

She tried to stay focused on her salsa, but her mind kept wandering. With her phone sitting not too far from her on the counter, Aria's eyes flicked back and forth from it to her work, waiting for a notification to pop-up.

Meanwhile, Lucy hopped off of I-75 at 9 Mile Road and entered the home stretch of her commute. She had a bemused smile on her face, thick tortoise-shell shades over her eyes, and her brown hair lightly flipped in the wind that gusted through the open sunroof of her little red sporty coupe. Dressed in subtly pinstriped slacks and a sleeveless cream-colored blouse, her jacket was hung up on a hanger in the backseat. It was such a beautiful Friday afternoon and Lucy felt on top of the world after a great week at work. The dance pop music coming from the car stereo made it all the better.

After a few more turns, Lucy felt a renewed sense of

excitement as she pulled up into the driveway. The house was cute and cottage-y, painted dark blue with white trim. Further up the driveway near the back of the house was a matching garage with its door open, holding Aria's older sedan. Lucy drove up behind it and put her car in park. She turned the key and the car quieted, and then she stepped out into the summer air. Smiling to herself, she took her jacket and bag from the backseat and then Lucy made her way to the side door of the house.

She entered through the kitchen, and upon coming in she saw Aria standing there at the counter, slicing into a bell pepper. Aria turned her head and saw Lucy, and her smile grew big and bright. She set her knife down, wiped her hands off, and then hurried over to where Lucy stood. Aria wrapped her arms around Lucy's neck, and the two kissed deeply and excitedly.

"Happy Friday!" cooed Aria, nuzzling her nose against Lucy's. Lucy laughed and quickly stole another kiss.

"It's good to be home," replied Lucy. "But forgot about that. Your news!"

"Nothing yet," Aria said, slumping down. "I'm supposed to get an email today but it's almost five and I haven't heard anything."

"Don't worry, babe," Lucy consoled. "If it doesn't come in today, I'm sure you'll hear Monday. And I'm sure it'll be good news."

"I hope so," Aria bemoaned with a pouting look. Lucy chuckled softly and kissed her.

"I love you," Lucy said.

"I love you, too."

The girls embraced tightly and leaned into each other.

Aria returned to her salsa, and after Lucy dropped her things in the adjoining room, she came back into the kitchen and took a can of sparkling water from the refrigerator. Cracking the can open, she took a sip and then smiled as she watched Aria work. Less than a year ago, Lucy left New York and moved home to Michigan. Back then, she never could have imagined she'd be standing right here, right now. She had a great new job, she had a house, and she was in love. Whatever bumps she had endured, they were worth it.

Then, out of nowhere, Aria's phone buzzed. Both she and Lucy's eyebrows lifted quickly and Aria, without even wiping her hands off this time, picked up her phone and began furiously tapping into it. She jumped into her email and saw the new message.

"It's here!" she called out. "It's an attachment. Ahh!"

Lucy laughed.

"Okay, so open it!"

Aria quickly tapped into her screen and waited for the letter to load. Then she focused, with a look of seriousness on her face as she read the letter, eyes full of excitement. Lucy waited with bated breath.

"I'm in," Aria said simply. She looked up at Lucy and her smile grew. "I got in. I got in!"

"Congratulations!" Lucy beamed with glee. She leaped forward and hugged Aria.

"I can't believe it," Aria went on, hugging Lucy as they

stood there in the kitchen. "I'm in nursing school at Wayne State. I'm going to be a nurse. That's amazing."

"I can believe it," offered Lucy. "Your grades from your first bachelors were good. You've got great letters of recommendation. And with your transfer credits taking care of your gen ed requirements, it should only take you two years to complete the degree. You're going to be a nurse."

Aria smiled brightly, and so did Lucy. They hugged yet again. There was real love between them, something special, something unique. They had both been put through the wringer, but they were coming out on the other side renewed and hopeful. There was a light at the end of the tunnel and they were reaching for it together.

"And with that," said Lucy. "I'm going for a run!" Lucy jokingly posed in a runner's stance and Aria laughed.

Aria's laugh then faded into a big silly grin, still gripping tightly to her phone. She was ecstatic.

LATER ON, after dinner, Lucy took her evening shower and washed the week off of her. It was nice to be back in the office, furthering her career, and feeling accomplished. Although it was a bit strange to be working with Paul, who was now her soon-to-be step-father, the awkwardness of the situation was fading and Lucy was starting to feel comfortable in her new position. It had been almost six months since she started at the company, and in that time she had shown what she was capable of. Her coworkers were noticing, and this gave her hope. Her previous loss was just a blip, and her stock was on the rise.

Now dressed in pink satin shorts and a matching camisole, Lucy stepped lightly down the stairs and into the living room. Aria was sitting there on the couch, drinking a mocktail of cranberry juice and seltzer, and when she saw Lucy her eyes lit up. She, too, was dressed down for the night, wearing just a long gray v-neck t-shirt and nothing else. Her blonde hair was up in a loose bun. Aria smiled and blew a kiss at Lucy.

"There room on the sofa for me?" Lucy asked with a teasing sparkle in her eye.

"Of course," Aria replied, patting the seat next to her. Lucy plopped down and cuddled against her. They kissed.

"Everything looks really nice in here," offered Lucy, giving the room a scan. "You did a good job organizing and moving things today."

"I couldn't help it," conferred Aria with a laugh. "I was so anxious all day about getting that email. I was trying to keep myself busy."

"Oh, I definitely understand that feeling," said Lucy. "I've been there."

"I just feel... so happy," admitted Aria. "I've always tried to stay optimistic and have a positive attitude, but I've had some rough times. It wasn't always easy. But now... it just feels like everything is on a good track, you know? I feel like my life is truly beginning. And I'm so happy that I get to share it all with you."

Lucy smiled, feeling touched, and she kissed Aria deeply.

As Lucy was pulling back from the kiss, Aria leaned in and kissed her a few more times, placing her hand on Lucy's thigh and giving it a squeeze. Lucy moaned softly into Aria's mouth.

"You know how much I like my thigh squeezed," cooed Lucy softly. Aria grinned.

"Yes, I do."

"How do you like it?" Lucy asked seductively. She put her hand on Aria's thigh and squeezed just as she had. Aria laughed and then grinned.

"Up higher," Aria provoked.

"Here?" Lucy replied, moving her hand up Aria's leg.

"Higher still."

"Oh," offered Lucy, heeding Aria's command. "Like this?" She moved her hand underneath Aria's sleep shirt and rested it right at the top her her thigh.

"Yeah, but you're a little off," Aria teased. "Now you've got to move it down and in." Lucy laughed.

"I can do that," said Lucy. She did as she was told and then she looked surprised. "You're not wearing any underwear."

"Nope," Aria confirmed. "I am not."

Lucy laughed again and then, as her hand began to rub against Aria's middle, fingers running over the short hair between Aria's legs, she pressed herself into Aria and resumed their kiss. It was full and affectionate, and the passion between them grew still. Since moving in together, their flame had truly ignited. And it continued to burn bright, growing stronger every day.

Life doesn't always follow the trajectory that one might hope, and there will always been valleys among one's peaks. The key is perseverance and to not give up hope. Even if everything appears to be crumbling, even if one find's themselves in a hole that looks insurmountable, there is always a way through. Life isn't a straight line, nor is it without its pitfalls and setbacks. There was a time Lucy felt hopeless, like she had lost all of her momentum, like she had lost everything. But it wasn't the end of the world. It was only the beginning.

You have to press on through to see what's waiting for you on the other side. Do not despair, do not curse the hard times because they are what make us who we are. There is love and success out there for us all, but it is up to us to define what that means in our own lives. Perhaps the path to success you originally envisioned was not the path you were ever on. Sometimes a change is in order to really see the light.

Aria fell back into bed, and Lucy slowly moved down the length of her body. She kissed each of Aria's nipples, she kissed her stomach, and then she kissed further down still. Aria raised her arms up and pushed her hands underneath the pillows, her legs widening as she anticipated what was next. And Lucy grinned happily as she gazed at what lay before her. She licked once, and then again, and then she buried her mouth against Aria, kissing her deeply, pressing her face into her lover's heat.

Lucy felt whole. She was home. Her old life in New York had been just a step, it was not the end of the line for her.

Here with Aria, this was where Lucy knew she was supposed to be. And here she would stay. Lucy wanted nothing more than to be with Aria always. Together, Lucy and Aria could take on anything. Together, their future was bright. This kind of love made it all worth it, and on that they could both agree.

If you want to be notified
of all new releases from Nico,
sign up for her mailing list today
and get 3 FREE BOOKS!

Point your web browser
to the following address
and sign up right now!

www.nicolettedane.com

Keep reading to see more books from
Nicolette Dane!

DIRTY JOB

Mallory Hunt has made a name for herself as "Lory Lick," a professional cam girl who posts videos of herself online in every position she can think up. She films herself solo and in the comforts of her apartment in Chicago, earning a great living and trying to achieve her dream of leaving the city for good. Her job is dirty, but it's also fun and lucrative.

Searching for another girl to join her to appease her fans, Mallory meets Jessi Chappell. Jessi is intrigued by Mallory's openness, and despite her own insecurities she decides to take Mallory up on her offer. But working with someone who makes dirty videos for a living can be a confusing ride when intimacy is so disconnected from a roll in the sheets.

As Jessi grows closer to Mallory, she discovers that this sensual provocateur is much more than she lets on. Could what these girls have together be the real deal, or is it all just for the camera?

Follow The Link To See More

www.nicolettedane.com

POCKET QUEENS

Constance Duke is a professional Texas Hold'em player. She's sharp and stoic, with a steely poker face and a drive to win. The regulars at her local poker room fear her, and the casuals underestimate her at their own peril. Constance is happy making a good living playing poker on her terms. And then she meets Mina Frye.

Mina is a gifted pickpocket, cunning and conniving, and equally charming and beautiful. At first, Mina sees Constance as just another mark. But she quickly realizes that Constance has much greater potential, and as the two begin to fall for one another, Mina convinces her that Las Vegas and the Poker World Championship are calling Constance's name.

As Constance competes with the world's best poker players, moving her way up in the tournament, she must also navigate the secrets of Mina's checkered past in Las Vegas. The magic they both feel is undeniably real, but is everything with Mina just a bluff to trick Constance into going all-in?

Follow The Link To See More

www.nicolettedane.com

TRAIL BLAZER

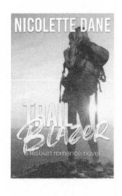

As her birthday approaches, Gretchen Slate is looking to do something big. Gretchen is an avid hiker, a lover of the outdoors, and sets her sights on Maine's 100 Mile Wilderness, an arduous and remote hike far away from civilization. And she can think of no better company than her best friend Naomi Benson.

This hike is known to change people, and Naomi is in need of a change. She's never left home, never applied herself, and never admitted her true feelings for Gretchen. In fact, Naomi has spent her life running away from her feelings. While Gretchen is eager to get into the woods and climb mountains, Naomi has her own inner mountains to climb.

Out in the wild, it's easy to open up and be your real self. Can these two friends bring the love they feel in the wilderness with them when they return home?

Follow The Link To See More

www.nicolettedane.com

Mae Huxley runs a budding tech start-up in Detroit, with the mission of getting more girls into computer programming. But she's hit a snag. In the midst of a new project that promises to spread her teachings worldwide, Mae and her business are running out of money.

Through a bit of serendipity, Mae is connected with one of her idols—wealthy technology goddess Audrey Addison. Audrey worked for the biggest tech giant out there, and now she owns her own angel investment firm. But she's a serious and severe woman, a keen business mind, and she's known to be an ice queen despite her fiery red hair.

As they grow the company together, Mae sees through Audrey's stern reputation and discovers the real woman underneath. Can Mae melt Audrey's heart and succeed both in business and in love?

Follow The Link To See More
www.nicolettedane.com

LADY PILOT

Captain Elaine Cole is an accomplished and popular commercial airline pilot. She's spent her entire career bouncing from one airport to the next, and one lover to the next as well. Being a pilot has made it hard for Lanie to settle down and find love, and now that she's in her forties it's really starting to wear on her.

When Carrie Haden is assigned as a flight attendant on her route, Lanie feels herself falling for the beautiful younger woman. But Carrie is different than the flight attendants Lanie has been with in the past. There's something else there—a brighter spark, a deeper affection—and Lanie can't help but feel that this is her opportunity to finally find the love she seeks.

Building trust and committing to a relationship is difficult for a pilot like Lanie. Could Carrie be the one who finally inspires Lanie to change her ways?

Follow The Link To See More
www.nicolettedane.com

AN EXCERPT: DIRTY JOB

The screen was all black. Slowly, modern-styled white lettering began to fade in and reveal the title of the video that was playing. The onscreen text read, "Lory Lick Presents... A Real Girlfriend Experience." And then the text faded out and the picture faded in. It was a smiling young woman, early to mid thirties with a bright and perky visage. She had dark brown hair that she wore in a braid that fell over one shoulder, and she was looking natural without any makeup. This woman was pretty, and just the image of her there on the screen was enticing and inviting.

As her image came into full view, it was obvious that she

was lying in bed. All that could be seen of her body was her bust, and she wore a purple strapless bra with a small bow between the cups. She had a small chest, and was slim and lithe. The camera mainly focused on her face, which remained smiling and jubilant, and it was close enough to her that it could have been the woman herself that was holding it.

"Hey baby," she said in a sultry voice. "I've missed you so much. I hate that work takes you away from me all the time, and I've been thinking... just because we can't be intimate in real life, that doesn't mean we can't be intimate."

The camera panned down a bit, and the woman began to rub her hand over one of her breasts, fondling it through her bra. Seductively, she peeled the cup down slightly, almost revealing her nipple, but she released the fabric before showing anything further.

"I think about you so much when you're away," she continued. "And now I want to show you what I do in bed when I'm thinking about you."

Her eyes looked away from the camera for a moment and she smiled longingly, as though she really were thinking about you. And then, after another beat, her eyes returned to looking straight into the camera.

"I want to show you what I do with that toy you bought for me," she said. "I want to show you how it makes me feel. But first..."

Sitting up straighter, the woman reached a hand behind her back and unclipped the clasp of her bra. Bringing both hands to her chest, she placed her palms on the cups and took hold of it, slowly beginning to peel it off of her. It took her sometime to complete this action, pulling the bra down until she finally revealed her breasts. They were small, but both nipples were pierced with barbells. She took the bra and set it down on the bed next to her. Then, looking back to the camera, she offered a simple smile and she shook her chest a few times, causing her tits to jiggle just slightly.

"Do you like my titties?" she asked, looking down at her chest. She gripped one of her breasts and squeezed it. "I know they're small, but I really love them. I hope you love them, too."

The woman adjusted herself and perched on her knees, squaring her shoulders to push out her chest. She looked back and forth from the camera to her chest, offering a few more shakes, some firm rubbing, and she flicked the barbell on one of her nipples.

"I can be self-conscious about them sometimes," she said. "But I remember when you told me... 'Lory, I love your tits.' And you kissed me. That really meant a lot to me. Let me show you how much you mean to me."

Lory moved around unhurriedly, reframing herself in the shot so that most of her body could now be seen. She wore panties that matched her discarded bra, and she slipped one of her hands into them. Carefully, she pushed them down over her ass and hips, and then she folded over to allow herself to take them down her legs and pull them off her feet. She smiled sensually and then tossed the purple panties away. Now she was fully naked, positioned half-sitting and half-laying in bed. Lory had a nice body. Her stomach was toned, with the slightest hint of abs becoming visible. Between her legs was just a thin strip of hair. She was as manicured as this experience was manicured.

"Oh, I almost forgot," said Lory. "I want to show you something else."

Turning around now, Lory presented her backside to the camera and she bent down on the bed so that her ass took up much of the screen. Reaching back, she peeled her cheeks apart to show that she was wearing a jeweled plug in her ass, shimmering purple in color that matched her removed lingerie. From this angle, everything could be seen. Lory's entire underside was immaculately waxed. Her pussy was pink and glistening with a subtle wetness, her folds looking delicate and soft. Her sex was curated. She knew exactly what she was doing.

"Do you like my plug?" Lory asked, turning her head back to face the camera. "I like to wear it out in public sometimes and think about you."

She shook her ass a few times, and then reached a hand back and gave a pull on the plug. Then she pulled a little harder, so that not just the stainless steel stem of it could be seen, but also the bulbous plug itself, stretching her ass and coaxing it open just slightly. Then Lory released it, causing everything to snap back in place.

"It feels so good inside me," she purred.

And then she hit the spacebar on her laptop, causing the video to pause. Sitting at the dining room table in her small kitchen in her Chicago apartment, Mallory Hunt sat up straighter in her chair and took a sip of tea from her mug. She was dressed in her pajamas, a thin camisole and soft pants, and she looked into the screen as though she were lost in thought.

Any embarrassment she had ever felt from looking at her own ass on video had melted away some time ago. Now she simply wanted it to look as perfect as she could make it. She wasn't all that happy with the lighting in this scene, but it would have to do. Pumping out videos like this was a churn, and she could only afford to be somewhat persnickety. The dim lighting and that single hair she noticed would have to do.

Mallory had watched this video a handful of times to make sure it was up to her growing standards. The edits and tweaks she made were small, barely noticeable to her intended audience, but she always noticed. It was difficult to let it go sometimes. But she knew that if she didn't get this video out by tonight, she might see her income dwindle. And she knew that her occasional mental health breaks would tear her away from her videos for weeks at a time, and it always helped to have a growing library of content to soften the blow. She always planned to have a few videos waiting in the wings for those down times, but Mallory was never able to get ahead of herself to make that happen.

"Hmm," Mallory released in a sigh, eyes still focused on her own ass onscreen. She liked her butt, but she thought it could be a little tighter.

When she started this journey—becoming a cam girl

and porn video creator—Mallory had no idea what she was doing. She just jumped into it, essentially making video after video of fingering herself to orgasm in different parts of her apartment. But she had grown as an actress, and she found herself pushing her own envelope more and more, trying different stuff to see how it made her feel. It was a lonely job, so spicing it up and adding some variation was a must. Her toy collection had become impressive, and her dedication to fitness had grown substantially. Whenever she saw more definition in her abs on camera, she felt really good about herself.

And Mallory had much bigger goals in life. She often had to remind herself of that whenever she got depressed or exhausted from her work. The money from her sex videos was great, and it was bringing her closer to the life that she wanted. In that way, she felt extremely fortunate to have the opportunity to make money the way she did. She got to sell sex, safely from the comfort of her home, all by herself, without any of the downsides of a more mainstream porno career. Mallory had the skills to make that happen for herself. She knew she was a lucky woman.

But it was lonely and it did get hard. It could be a dirty job, and it wasn't always fun and trouble-free. Mallory could feel one of those bouts of depression coming on, and she knew she had to finish this video now, publish it, announce it to her fans, and then close her laptop for a few days in an effort to make sense of everything that was happening to her and to the world around her. Sometimes it was too much to bear.

She hit the spacebar and the video started back up again.

"Do you want to pull it out?" her voice asked through the speakers of her laptop. "Go slow, okay?"

Follow The Link To See More

www.nicolettedane.com

Thank you for reading!

If you enjoyed this novel,
please leave a review!

Reviews are *super* important!
Your review can help Nico
reach more readers!

Even if you're not the wordy type,
leaving a review saying
"I really enjoyed this book!"
is still incredibly helpful.

Pretty please?

Made in the USA
Coppell, TX
12 February 2021

50275194R00152